I0683051

The Ultimate Catch

Constance Phillips

Published by: Constance Phillips Press

Copyright, 2014 – all rights reserved

ISBN 13: 978-0692520079
ISBN 10: 0692520074

© Constance Phillips 2013. All Rights Reserved

Editor: Dave Field

Cover artist: Kim Jacobs, Calliope-designs

All rights are reserved. No part of this book may be used or reproduced in any manner without written permission.

This book is a work of fiction. The names, characters, places, and incidents are products of the author's imagination or have been used fictitiously and are not to be construed as real. Any resemblance to persons, living or dead, actual events, locale or organizations are entirely coincidental.

DEDICATION

This book is dedicated to those who reach for the stars, do what they must, and don't let anything get in their way.

ACKNOWLEDGMENTS

As always thank you to my husband and my children. You are the best support system I could ever ask for.

I would never get through the hours of writing alone, without my support crew. Thanks to the B-I-C Crew. Specifically, Shay Lacy, Jenna Rutland, Sloan Parker, Jayne Kingston, and Jill Kemerer for keeping me on track and encouraging me to keep pushing forward. Thank you Kathy Satterlee and Mary Kenton for your support and encouragement.

CHAPTER ONE

Jolanda cupped the short, wide glass in her hand. The smell of cheap whiskey sent her stomach into another medal-worthy, gymnastic tumble. She leveled her gaze, focusing on the Nordic-looking captain of the *Sydney* standing on the opposite side of the mahogany bar, ever mindful of her movements. If she shifted too fast she'd hurl the previous five shots, costing her the bet. "Let me on your crew, Keller."

"You haven't won, yet." His clenched teeth signaled confidence, but she could see cracks in his armor. He swayed to the right and his shot glass rattled as he misjudged the distance between his hand and the bar top.

If Keller broke down, she would snatch the opening.

A balloon payment was coming due on her father's house. Had he been able to fish for crab as he had every winter for more than twenty years, the debt would be paid on time, but a quarter century of hard living had left his health as broken down as the mortgaged home.

Out of control diabetes and blood pressure had forced him into retirement.

Some might say he'd given his best years to that boat, but Jo liked to think he'd spent that time with her. Despite a nasty divorce, Lark had never let anger or frustration taint his relationship with his daughter. He fished in the winter while she was at her mother's house in Fairbanks, so he could be a father during the summer when she lived with him.

Lifting the shot glass to her lips and gripping the edge of the bar with her free hand, she tipped her head back hoping the amber liquid would bypass her taste buds and glide down her throat.

Mission failed.

A cough pressed against her esophagus, but Jo pushed back with her iron will, refusing to open the door to the puking that would give Keller the victory.

The only way to win the spot on the boat was to out-drink its captain.

Whose idea was this? That's right: mine.

At five foot two, Jo weighed a hundred and fifteen pounds soaking wet. When she drank, it was never more than a half glass of white wine with dinner. These fishermen guzzled bourbon same as water. As drunk as she was, she could still see Keller was six feet of solid muscle: gorgeous, chiseled muscle.

Whoa! Keller? Handsome?

That had to be the whiskey talking!

The second job as a bartender at the Elbow Room was a Hail Mary attempt to help raise the needed money. Very few of the bar's patrons—fishing boat's crews—lived here in the small town of Unalaska, or even the state of Alaska. They breezed in and fished from the Bering Sea, made obscene amounts of money off their bounty, and jetted back to the Pacific Northwest to spend the riches on their families and in their communities, leaving behind a small town dependent on the fisheries.

"You ready to give up yet?" Keller's words clung to a raspy cough. He tried to lock the gaze from his blood-shot, blue eyes to hers, but they circled and swayed off track. His normally pale flesh was getting green around the gills. Maybe she had a chance to win.

She picked the bottle up off the bar, and refilled the glasses. "Let me on your boat."

An arm came around her, grabbing the bottle. She leaned back against the familiar, firm chest and looked up into her lifelong friend's eyes.

"Enough. This is over. I'm taking you home," Graham said.

How did he get behind the bar?

"I can't. I'm still on the clock."

He laughed as he released his grip on the bottle, but still held her close. "Ralph clocked you out an hour ago, when you started this stupid bet." Graham glanced across the bar to his boss. "Come on. This is insane. She's going to get sick."

Jo broke free of Graham's hold and stumbled forward, grabbing her glass. "Are you ready?"

Keller gripped the counter. "I admire your father. He's worked hard for me and my family. But, you know better than anybody the superstitions about letting women fish."

"Really? You believe in that crap?"

"It doesn't matter what I believe. My crew thinks there's something to the lore. I'd lose them if I let you work on my boat." He stumbled back as he tossed the whiskey into his mouth.

She braced herself and drank. The glass rattled again as it hit the bar, but she focused on her center.

Stay down. Stay down.

"I thought you were the captain. Aren't you man enough to make the decisions?"

"I have to think about everyone who's counting on me to have a good season. I'm responsible for the life and livelihood of each person on my boat." He leaned in

4

so close that all she could focus on was his thin, pink lips, wondering how they'd taste.

Her fingers tangled in the long strands of black hair falling in her face as she pushed it back over her shoulder. She reminded herself that it was only the copious amount of booze that made Keller look like a scrumptious steak she'd like to devour. "And you call my people superstitious?"

"Don't do that. You know this isn't about that."

Why had she brought the fact she was Aleut into this? It had to be her dead grandmother speaking through her. Nana warned her father not to marry Elle Anderson because of the cultural differences, and the old woman had taken an uncanny pleasure in being right when Mom left Dad and later settled in Fairbanks with her new husband.

"I can do the work."

"You don't even know what you're signing up for."

That wasn't true. "I've been around it all my life."

"No. You father has. Graham has. I have. Not you. You weren't anywhere near a boat."

"Give me a shot." She cringed at the whiney sound of her voice. It didn't really matter that the alcohol was to blame, the last thing she wanted to do was beg.

"You're so tiny! I bet you'd have trouble lifting a five pound bag of sugar, let alone a twenty-five pound box of frozen herring."

"I might be small, but I'm not afraid of hard work."

"Let me loan you the money."

Why was it so hard for the men her life to understand she didn't want a handout? "I don't want to trace one debt for another!"

"When your father comes back to work next season, we'll work something out."

These fishermen were all the same. Next season. Next trip. Next time. Never once did they stop to think about a plan B. She tapped her fingernails against the bar, trying to expel her frustration. "He's not coming back! He's never going to be able to fish again. Besides, a Gilles always earns their way." She picked up the bottle and refilled both the glasses.

Keller grabbed her wrist. "I can't drink any more and neither should you."

Victory!

"If you're giving up, then I win."

"I'm not."

"Then drink."

He lifted the shot glass to his mouth, then pushed it away and twisted his head to the side. After taking two ragged breaths, he tossed it back and dropped the glass. His stare pierced through her and she watched his chest rise and fall as the light in his eyes faded. Without warning, he spun away from the bar, bent at the waist, and retched. The seven shots of whiskey spilled from his gut, mixing with the sawdust on the wood floor.

"You lost! You have to hire me." She expected to be more excited, but the haze of inebriation kept her in a cloud. Did her voice have the conviction she wanted? She needed? Hopefully Keller didn't see that the putrid smell of his vomit was twisting her gut into knots.

He coughed and hacked, but didn't look back at her. "Not unless you drink one more and keep it down! If you can't, it's a draw. The deal was if you out-drank me."

One more drink. It was going to be hard enough without the sour smell making her head spin. Or was it the previous six shots doing that? She picked up the glass and focused on the one thing that mattered, saving her father's house.

He deserved the place to recover and retire. Lark might not be the tough-as-nails man of the sea he used to be, but the payoff for twenty-plus years of grueling work should be their home.

One more time she poured the whiskey down her throat. The sound of her empty glass hitting the bar rang out like a victory bell.

Keller's gaze bore down on her as if he was trying to force her to puke with his sheer will. She didn't look away, refused to let herself be pushed around by these clods. Mind over matter, she focused on her breathing.

In. Out. In. Out.

How had she never noticed how blue his eyes were before? Just when she thought she might have to look away, so as not to drown in those pools, he grabbed her wrist and guided her down the length of the bar to a quiet corner, blocking her with his solid frame. "Are you trying to ruin me?"

"No! I'm trying to save myself."

"Don't make me do this."

The booze gripped her stomach and clouded her mind. She felt herself sway and the white haze thicken between them. "How can you go back on your word? I won the bet. You have to give me the job."

He slid his left hand up her right arm leaving a trail of goose bumps behind his touch. As he gripped her shoulders, concern softened his emotions. "Are you all right?"

She averted her eyes, the mere closeness of him sending waves of arousal through her. Her father always joked about women looking better at closing time. It must work both ways. "Just tell me you're a man of your word. Dad always said the Sveinssons could be counted on. That you were virtuous."

"This isn't what you think. I'd do anything to help Lark."

"Then don't treat his daughter like shit!"

"This isn't personal. We're talking about my livelihood. I can't let you screw with that." The vein running down the side of his neck throbbed as the words passed through his lips, stretched thin and taught. Even though he was bordering on rage, all Jo could focus on was the passion he must have in order to feel anything with that much conviction.

"All I'm asking for is a chance to earn my way. I don't want to be handed anything."

Graham's voice filtered into her conscious and she followed it to the left of Keller. "Let me take you home before you do something else you end up regretting."

She waved her hand in front of her face, tipping her own balance to the left. "Leave me alone. You're not my keeper."

Graham moved in and caught her before she fell, wrapping an arm around her shoulder. Jo leaned on him for support. As always, she could count on him to protect her from herself.

He pushed her hair back over her shoulder. "Yeah, your father might have something to say about that. Come on. This is over."

Jo pushed herself out of Graham's arms and stumbled toward Keller. She couldn't leave the bar until she had his word. "So, what's it going to be?"

Keller hesitated and then swiped a hand across his chin. "What can I do? You won the bet. Be at the boat at six thirty in the morning with the rest of the crew."

Jo gave her weight to the wall and watched Keller amble back to the bar. Even though it took him two tries to get back up on the stool, the sight of him still made her dizzy. Or was that all the booze she'd drank?

Graham grabbed her forearm. "Let's get you outside before you puke."

He rambled on as he led her toward the bar, grabbed her coat from Ralph, and then continued toward the door. She reached for the handle, but Graham pulled her back, and helped her into her coat. After she zipped the front and wrapped the scarf tight around her neck, he held the door for her.

For the first time in two months, she felt like she could take a deep breath. Tomorrow she could go to the bank and arrange to pay off the loan. Her father wasn't going to lose the house. "Where are you parked?"

Graham leaned back against the building and shook his head. "You're not getting in my car yet."

"I want to go home." She sounded whiney, even to her own ears.

"I don't want you to barf in my car."

"The *car*. The only woman you'll ever love." She was joking. Kind of. Graham had paid more money than she could imagine spending on anything to have the classic car shipped to him from the lower forty-eight and didn't seem to value anything more than it.

"You can stand here for a few minutes in the crisp, cool air and get your wits about you."

She tried to stand straight, but the breeze was brushing against her, setting her off balance in her weakened state. Graham started to laugh, but then muttered a curse. After grabbing her shoulders and turning her, he leaned her back against the wall and then fished a pack of cigarettes out of his breast pocket. Pulling one from the box, he cupped his hand over the end and lit it.

"You need to stop that."

"What do you care if I smoke?"

"They'll kill you. I don't want to see you end up like my dad."

He leaned back and slowly exhaled the first drag. "Do you ever wonder if your dad is right?"

She could hear the door to the bar open and a group of patrons leaving. From the laughs and chiding she knew it was the crew of the *Sydney*, but didn't bother to turn to see if Keller was with them. She didn't want to give him an in to a conversation, a chance to recant the job offer.

Graham snapped his fingers in front of her face. "You with me?"

She shook off the haze. "Wonder if Dad is right about what?"

"About us? That we belong together."

She pushed her hand against his shoulder. "Shut up! And you think *I* drank too much?"

"Maybe it's not such a stupid idea." He pushed the cigarette back between his lips and rubbed his hands together for warmth.

She pulled the smoke from his mouth and squashed it beneath the heel of her boot. "You don't love yourself enough to quit abusing your body with this crap, why should I take you in? So I can take care of you when your way of life catches up to you?"

"What do you mean by that?"

"Fishermen! You are all alike. You don't know the meaning of home or family. Your first and only love is the sea."

Graham looked her in the eye, and she could see the wounds below his tough guy appearance. "You're wrong, you know. I think about the future all the time. I want a fairy-tale ending just as much as you."

"But not *with* me."

"You wouldn't have to work so hard."

She threw her arms in the air in frustration, but didn't have the heart to continue arguing with him. Graham was just trying to help. She knew that, but she didn't need charity from him or anyone else. When it came to the two of them, she was the responsible one. The one who kept the candle lit while the men in her life tempted the sea.

Besides, she knew when he woke up the next day, this sentimental moment would pass.

"I'm going to walk home."

She was half-way up the street before she heard Graham's heavy steps crunching against the snow. He grabbed her arm, and pulled her back. "Like hell, you are. With my luck you'd pass out in a snow bank and freeze to death."

"I can take care of myself and my father. I don't need you or anyone else to try and save me."

"I know you can, but you shouldn't have to."

CHAPTER TWO

Keller staggered down the steps to his quarters, still amazed he'd made the jump from dock to boat without landing in the harbor. Not that the gap was huge, but getting from his truck to the end of the pier had been chore enough.

Thank goodness for Fred. If not for his deck boss, Keller would be sleeping this one off in his truck in the parking lot behind the Elbow Room.

As he tripped over the threshold to his cabin, Fred called him back into the galley. "Whoa, buddy, one foot in front of the other. Left, right, left, right."

"Screw off." Keller leaned back against the wall. He already regretted the seven shots of whiskey that topped the three beers he'd ingested before making the stupid bet. Now, he wanted his bed, and for the whole evening to be a nightmare, not another weight trying to sink his boat. "Say what you need to, so I can go to bed."

"I don't think lying down's a good idea, unless you want to start puking again."

"There isn't anything left." Aside from the embarrassing end to his wager, he'd stopped on the corner just outside the bar to throw up again and had just finished a third round beside his truck. His stomach was empty.

Fred took his arm and shoved him toward the galley. "Regardless, you'll feel better with some eggs and sausage on that stomach."

Eating?

Keller desired that about as much as this little heart-to-heart talk that Fred seemed equally determined to make happen. Both hovered low on his want-to-do list, right under "have a colonoscopy" and above "poke yourself in the eye with a sharp, pointy stick." He didn't need all the reasons why Jolanda couldn't work on this boat enumerated. He'd already created a long and winding list all by himself.

Using the edge of the table to steady himself, he slid into the bench seat that rounded the corner of the galley. "How about a beer?"

"I'm starting some coffee."

Fred need not have announced his actions. Keller could hear the water running and the drawers and cupboards opening and closing, all amplified by the pain throbbing in his temples. He propped his elbows on the table and settled his head in his hands, struggling to grip his cropped hair.

A few moments later, the clanging ceased and the hiss and crackle of eggs, sausage, and potatoes frying assaulted him. To his surprise, the aroma of the food and strong coffee called him back to the land of the living.

"What are you going to do about the woman?" Fred asked.

"Jolanda?" Just saying her name caused a ping in Keller's heart. He couldn't remember a time that Lark didn't work for his father or that he hadn't known of Jo, but he'd never really taken notice of her before tonight. "What can I do? A bet is a bet."

"I still can't believe that little girl out-drank you."

Even if Lark always called her his baby, she was a full-fledged woman, with soft curves and a spine of steel. "She's not a child."

"I meant little as in small. She can't be more than five foot and skinny as a tow-line."

With beautiful brown eyes and long black hair.

"Do you know how much money your crew lost in side bets alone?"

Why was Fred still talking? Keller's stomach sloshed to the right and he swallowed the acids back down. His throat burned; his voice cracked. "That's what the dumbasses get for betting."

"It looked like a sure thing," Fred said. "Never mind the side bets, though. They can live without twenty or thirty bucks. They're more worried about the boat coming in with empty tanks and going home with empty wallets."

"Because I'm letting a woman fish?" Keller knew all the old superstitions and while he'd like to say he didn't cave to the old school ways, if his crew believed the boat and trip was cursed by her presence, it might as well be a fact.

"Pete's talking about trying to find a different boat."

"That's ridiculous. The *Sydney* has always made its quotas and the men have always gotten paid. Same for the *Melbourne*. Jo's presence isn't going to change that."

"Yes, there's always been a paycheck to be had. And for a green captain, you had a decent season last year. But it hasn't even been two years since your dad died. And everyone knows if that hadn't happened you'd still be down in Washington playing house."

"Watch where you're stepping." Some things weren't open for discussion on the boat. One was his father's heart-attack and the other was his failed relationship with Brie. Fred must have a brass pair to be bringing up both right now.

Ignoring his warning, Fred continued to rant. "This year your brother walked away. And I won't even mention the blown engine two years ago and the two extra trips to town last year."

"Funny. Sounds like you're mentioning it to me." Why was he doing this? Did Fred really believe Keller wasn't aware of his own recent history? Many hours that should have been spent sleeping were depleted rehashing the mistakes and regrets.

"Everyone knows this company isn't as stable as it used to be. Some even wonder how long it can last." Fred dropped the plate and the clatter sent a stabbing pain straight to Keller's temples. "You got the *Melbourne* going out with a captain who isn't family, for the first time ever."

One whiff and Keller's stomach did another back flip. He averted his eyes, and responded to Fred's summary of events. "The crew doesn't know shit. Reese doesn't want to do this anymore and the boat has to fish. I hired a good captain." Looking back down at the plate, he saw it heaping over with a big, traditional, at-sea breakfast. "I can't eat this."

"It may not feel like the right thing to do, but trust me, it is. Just like backing out on your deal with Jo."

Keller picked up the fork and chopped the sunny-side up eggs, mixing them in with the potatoes and onions before filling his fork and taking a bite.

His father would never go back on his word, but Hal Sveinsson wouldn't have gotten into a drinking game with a woman. He would never have let the company hemorrhage money the way it had since his death either. Keller swallowed hard, the food balling up in his throat with the guilt and regret. "We've taken some hits the last two years. Huge hits. I need a big season more than anyone else."

"So, why are you spitting at the fates by letting that girl on board?"

"I'd like nothing more than to have Lark at his usual post, but that isn't going to happen. We need a fifth man on this deck. You know that."

"The key word being 'man.'"

"I made a bet and I lost. A Sveinsson man is always true to his word."

Or he's not a man at all.

The rest of his father's favorite saying rang in his ear. Keller rubbed the back of his neck, trying to force away the problem by easing the tight muscles.

His dad would be so disappointed in him.

"Talk Reese into coming up for just one more season."

"No." Keller couldn't blame his brother for walking away from the Bering Sea, their boats, and the fishing company at the start of the season. Hell, he'd been down that road.

His love for a woman had convinced him he could be a better man than his father, one who was there for his soon-to-be wife and their future children. He'd no idea the price he'd have to pay for making such an arrogant and selfish choice.

It was only a couple of weeks later when his mother called him in tears, telling him his father had suffered a major heart-attack while at sea. The Coast Guard hadn't arrived in time to save him.

Never again would he walk away from everything his father had sacrificed for. The company was his legacy and he'd be damned if the ship sank while he sat in the captain's chair.

But, Keller had no business comparing himself to his father. Hal had sacrificed everything for his wife, Keller, Reese, and their four sisters. And how did Keller thank him? By spitting in his face and turning his back on the family legacy. Who was he to think he deserved a *normal* life? For A Sveinsson, being a fisherman was normal.

Keller would never be the man his father had been.

Brie proved that when she kicked him out of their apartment. Tonight, he'd proved it again by jeopardizing the future of the boat by playing games with Jo. When she'd suggested the contest as a way to prove she could hang tough with him and his crew, he'd been sure it was his perfect escape. He never believed she would actually beat him. Maybe that was what he deserved for trying to take the easy way out.

How would he live with himself if his business choices cost him the *F/V Sydney* and the *F/V Melbourne*?

"But with Reese—"

"We don't need my brother!" As the words passed his lips, guilt descended on him. He didn't want to resent his brother for leaving the future of the company on his shoulders. Reese aspired to live a dream that wasn't meant for either of them. Only he was bringing a child into the mix.

He should have taken notes when Keller's love life had gone up in flames instead of trying to out-do him.

"It would be better if we had him; then you could keep your promise by shoving Jo down in the galley to fix meals."

"I can't afford a sixth person on the payroll." Keller pushed the last forkful of food into his mouth. He hated to admit it, but Fred had been right about the meal making him feel better.

"Then tell her Reese called tonight needing a spot on a boat. No one could blame you for siding with family."

"Damn it, Fred! He's not coming back." Keller threw his fork. It ricocheted off the wall and landed in the sink, a shot he couldn't have made if he'd tried.

"Well, then, I don't know what to tell you." Fred shifted his weight and slumped back against the wall. "These guys are nervous. I can't guarantee they won't jump boats if you follow through and let Jo fish."

What was he going to do? Running the boat with four men and a woman was going to be bad enough, but the idea of losing Graham, Norm, and Pete scared the hell out of him. Keller took a deep breath, let it out slowly, and then sipped from his cup. "Tell the guys I want to have a meeting in the morning. I'll guarantee them the same money as last year, no matter how we do. If we do better, I'll pay better, but they won't make less."

A night in the bar had never made Keller this stupid before. Why had he said such a thing? What was he even promising?

He squirmed his way out of the booth and started for his bunk, but instead of turning to the right, he moved to the left and climbed the steps up to the wheelhouse. On the counter that lined the back wall and port side of the room, he found his open accounting books just as he had left them. Next to the book was a yellow legal pad with the long list of numbers in red ink trying to sort out if making quota equaled making a profit.

Last year's crab seasons had sustained themselves. This year salmon and cod had turned a profit, but herring ended up in the red. More than anything, he needed big profits out of King crab.

The numbers on the page blurred. A night's sleep was in order before he tried to find a way to increase his profit, but how could he sleep when he knew the company was on the line?

He pulled his cell phone out of his pocket and opened the app with his recent calls, pressing on the word "Mom."

It was only after a groggy hello crossed the line that he realized it was an obscene hour. "I'm sorry, Mom. I didn't realize how late it was."

"Or early—depends how you look at it," she said.

He could hear a rustling and concluded she was sitting up in bed.

"What's wrong?" she asked.

"It can wait until morning."

"If it could wait, you wouldn't have called me now," she insisted. "I'm up, talk to me, Son."

Leave it to her to dig right to the heart-of-the-matter. "I was wondering if you could call some of Dad's friends and acquire more quota for us."

She exhaled slowly and he could imagine the look of concern on her face. "I'm not sure that's a good idea. You've got about all you and the boats can handle. More quota equals more trips."

"I know how this works. It would also mean increased profit."

She adopted a stern tone, and he immediately knew he'd crossed a line with his sarcasm. "I know I am as new to accounting as you are to being a captain, but I've studied your father's books and I lived with him for a good number of years. The company belongs to you and Reese, but you've asked for my help and my input, so I'm going to speak my mind when I feel the need. I don't think this is a good time to expand."

"I'm not thinking about growing the business; I just don't want to drown in the damn debt!"

"It's how the seasons start. Expenses come before profits. You know this."

"Please, Mom. Would you make the calls for me?"

There was a long pause on the other end of the line, but Keller resisted the urge to push his mother again.

Finally, she said, "Is this really about making a profit?"

"What else would it be about?"

"Brie."

His fingers curled around the edge of the counter. "I do *not* want to talk about this. She's gone."

"For some reason you think that's your fault."

"Isn't it?"

"No. Honey, the right person for you will stand by your side in a time of need. You haven't wanted to hear this, but I'm going to say it anyway. She wasn't the right person for you."

CHAPTER THREE

The pops and cracks of the eggs sizzling in the pan banged around in Jo's throbbing head like a ringing gong. She flipped the two offenders over in the cast iron pan and turned off the flame underneath.

Over light. Just like every other morning since she turned thirteen, Jo took care of all the little things for her father when she was with him.

After pushing down the black lever on the toaster, she reached up for the Tylenol bottle from the cupboard, and downed two of them with a swig of sour orange juice.

The shrill ring of her cell phone sliced the air and drowned out the sound of the eggs. Her mother was on some roll. This was the third call in fifteen minutes. When would the lady take a hint?

The sound of her father's cane hitting the linoleum in the hallway alerted her to the fact it was time to break the news.

"Good morning." That wasn't cheerful enough. He'd know there was something wrong.

He hung the cane on the back of his chair and lowered himself to the seat. "You're up early, especially since you don't have to work."

She set a cup of black coffee in front of him and his blood testing kit. To look at him, you wouldn't guess him to be as sick as he was. Aside from the fact he leaned heavily on the cane these days. Years of hard physical labor had given him a muscular frame that didn't seem to age, except for the increasing amount of grey in his black hair.

Maybe that was the reason no one seemed to believe his retirement was necessary. "Check your sugar before you drink your coffee. Breakfast will be ready before you're done."

He gave the contraption on the table a belligerent stare before he went about following her orders. "What are your plans for the day, baby girl?"

She cringed. As much as she loved being daddy's special-and-only daughter, something had snapped in the last six months. She now hated the endearment. "Actually, I *do* have to work today, but I'll still meet you at your doctor's appointment. You can get yourself there, right?"

"If you tell Mr. Crandell—"

"Not at the cannery. Another job."

The blood monitor beeped, and then she heard the sound of plastic hitting the table. "My blood count's fine. And you work too hard. All day in the cannery, four nights a week at that bar—which I still hate—and now what?"

"When the bills are paid—"

His coffee cup hit the table with more force than necessary. "They're *my* bills! Not your concern."

She'd done it now. He was angry. If she hadn't heard it in his voice, she could see all the signs on his face. His lips drawn so tight they'd almost disappeared and his eyes narrowed at her. Hoping it would blow over, Jo continued as usual, setting the plate in front of him. She then picked up the monitor and looked at the reading.

"This is *not* fine. Why do you say it's fine when it's not?" She spun half way around and opened the refrigerator. One good thing about a kitchen this small: there weren't many wasted steps.

How in the world was she going to spend four weeks out on a boat? Her father would never manage his medication on his own. Last weekend was proof enough of that. While she was up in Fairbanks at her mother's, he ate whatever he pleased, and skipped half of his doses of insulin.

And the trip was all for naught.

"The insulin doesn't do a damn thing. And don't change the subject. I'm not done talking about you working all the time. What happens with my mortgage isn't your concern."

She pulled an empty chair around next to him and laid a hand on his thigh. "*You're* my concern. I'm not going to let you lose this house." Holding the insulin pen up to the light, she twisted the knob on the top until it was at the right dose.

She handed the pen to him. "Or do you want me to do it?"

He nodded once and lifted the edge of his t-shirt.

Jo could see through the hard shell and tough guy image. He played as if the bills didn't bother him because he couldn't admit to having no way to pay them, and tried to ignore the doctors because he didn't want to believe his body was failing him.

After wiping his stomach with the alcohol swab, she stabbed him with the pen.

"That hurts." A huge smile pushed up his cheeks as he rubbed the spot, telling Jo he was trying to lighten the mood.

"Well, I'd give you a lollipop but you can't have one," she teased. "How about a sugar-free candy?"

"I'd rather have a ginger-snap." The humor in his voice disappeared as fast as it had shown itself.

"Eat your breakfast," she whispered, reminding herself she should be gentler. All the changes to his diet in the last couple of months hadn't been easy. Lark didn't mean to hurt her or himself, he was simply frustrated. Anyone would be.

Her phone started ringing again. Pretending not to hear it, she picked up a piece of toast off his plate and bit into the corner.

"Your phone."

"I'm not deaf."

"Then are your hands broke? Answer it."

"I'm not speaking to her right now."

"Goodness, Jo. And you call *me* a child. I don't know what happened between you and your mother last weekend, but you need to get over it. If you don't, she's going to start calling me. One of the joys of being divorced is not having to listen to her yell."

For some twisted reason, that brought a smile and a chuckle. Probably because she knew he didn't mean any of it. Yes, her mother would eventually call him if Jo continued to give her the silent treatment, but she knew Lark would welcome an excuse to talk to Elle.

The divorce had been the hardest thing he'd ever lived through, and she believed part of him still held a torch for her. Sure, other women had come and gone over the years, but none had successfully made a place for themselves in his heart.

She leaned in, laid her arms over his shoulders and kissed his cheek. "I'll call her later. I have to get ready for work."

"You haven't told me where you're working yet."

Like a dog with a bone. It didn't matter that she was twenty-three years old; she wasn't going to slip out of this house until Daddy knew where she was going and when she'd be back.

The *Sydney*. Two simple words, so why wouldn't they break free from her throat? The front door slammed, interrupting her concentration. And her father's too.

Lark spun toward the other room. "Graham? Is that you?"

That light in her father's eye gnawed at her as if he was twisting the point of a fishing knife in her chest. Of course it was Graham. He was the only other person who walked in the house without knocking. The son Lark had always wanted, and the only guy her father would ever see as good enough for her.

"Come sit down, Son."

Graham breached the doorway of the kitchen. "You're not ready yet? Come on. I'm not taking any of Keller's shit because of you."

Lark's head snapped back to his daughter. "Are you working for Keller today? Doing what?"

Graham turned one of the kitchen chairs around and sat down, leaning forward against the back. "She didn't tell you, Pops?"

"Jo?" Lark's glare demanded an answer.

"I'm going out for king with them."

"The hell you are! What in the world is wrong with that boy? His father dies and he loses his damn mind!"

Lark reached for his cane and tried to pull himself to his feet. "No baby girl of mine is going out on a crab boat."

"In case you haven't noticed, I'm a grown woman and not your baby anymore. Someone has to pay off the mortgage."

"*My* mortgage. Not yours. Why can't you get that through your head? Graham, grab my boots and coat for me. There isn't any way in hell I'm letting my daughter go out on a boat when I'm fully able."

"Sir," Graham stumbled over the words. "I'm sorry, but you know the doctor is right. Your foot isn't well enough for you to go out this year."

Jo took her father's elbow, and pried the cane from his fingers before helping him back down to the chair. She clasped his hands in hers. "I can do this, Dad. Have some faith in me, okay. Just a few weeks and I'll be able to pay off the loan. Then I'll go back to just one job at the cannery, and you can focus on enjoying your retirement."

Lark covered his eyes with his hand and shook his head. "I ought to go down there and throttle that fool. What kind of idiot puts a woman on a fishing boat?"

"I'm going to ignore how sexist that remark is," Jo said before giving Graham her full attention. "Two minutes to get dressed and I'll be ready to go."

* * * *

Jo slipped into the pristine '67 Corvette Graham had paid way too much money for and winced when the door slammed. She watched her friend's face as he backed out of the driveway. Silence. He was pissed. On an average day, it'd bother her to have Graham angry, but right now she was just as mad.

After a long moment, Graham finally broke the silence. "Why did you leave me alone with your father?"

"So I could get dressed."

"You know how he is with his game of twenty questions. I always lose."

Her stomach went into a free fall. "What did you tell him?"

Graham tapped the center of the steering wheel with his knuckle. "About why you're mad at your mother. Why didn't you tell him about asking her for money?"

"I didn't want his pride to get in the way. I knew he'd hate taking money from Mom and Allen. What I didn't expect was for Mom to refuse."

"How could you think she'd say yes? Obviously your step-dad would have a problem with his wife giving money to her ex."

Jo lifted her right foot up, laying it on her left knee and twisted her head to look out the window. She'd been working hard to push the fight with her mother out of her mind all week, because thinking about it made her want to cry. "I didn't ask for dad, I asked for me. Allen always says he thinks of me as his own daughter. I guess he proved that's not true."

"I know I wouldn't be jumping to pay off my wife's ex-husband's mortgage. Just try to look at it from their side." Graham paused at the four-way stop, but instead of looking at her, he turned his head, and tapped his finger against the window. After a longer than necessary wait, he inched out into the intersection. The silence was deafening, and said a lot more than his words ever could.

"What are you so mad about?"

"Geez, Jo. Really? You made a fool out of yourself last night trying to out-drink Keller."

"Me? I'm not the one who puked on my shoes."

"And you're damn lucky you didn't do it in this car either." He shot her a sideways glance and his lips curved up just enough to reassure her that any anger was just on the surface.

Reaching between her legs, she picked up her purse and dug around until she found a brush. As she pulled it through the strands of her hair, she continued. "I think I passed out about two minutes after I stumbled through the door."

His focus turned back to the road as he drove. "You have no idea what you're setting yourself up for. You don't know what it's like. And what about after? What's going to happen when you don't show up at the cannery today?"

She twisted her hair up and secured it with a clip before covering it with a bean cap. "I'm off today, but I have to go talk to Mr. Crandell when we're done on the boat. I'm going to ask for a leave of absence."

"He'll fire you. With the shortage of good jobs around here, he'll have a replacement hired before you're out of the building."

She wanted to argue, but a piece of her suspected the same thing. "It'd be his loss."

"That might be true, but what are you going to do without that job? Tend bar at the Elbow Room for tips? You're better than that."

Despite Graham's sharp tone, she knew him well enough to know he yelled because he was scared. "My whole life, Dad's been there for me. This house, my home, I can't let the bank take it."

"You could move to Fairbanks, like your mom has begged you to do since you graduated. They've offered to help you pay for college and there's more work up there. Your brother and sister would love having you close."

She shrugged and looked away from him. A solid home where mommy and daddy came home every night for dinner, she'd longed for that when she was a kid, but those days were long gone. She wanted the kind of marriage and home life for herself someday, but it wouldn't be right to abandon her father for it. "Dad needs me to take care of him."

"You don't really believe that. Do you? Lark is perfectly capable of caring for himself."

"He's sicker than you know. Sicker than he looks."

"Pete, Norm, and Fred are going to make your life miserable, and by extension, mine. Do you know that?"

Jo's stomach flipped, and it wasn't from the aftereffects of drinking this time. Graham had always been a constant in her life; the one friend who remained true even when she disappeared for months at a time to live with her mom. He was a shoulder to lean on and he always took in stride the chiding from her father about the two of them being the perfect couple.

Well, except for the out-of-character suggestion he'd made about the two of them last night.

He deserved a lot better than she'd been giving him the last few days. "I didn't push to get on the boat to hurt you. I don't expect you to risk your own job to defend me or anything."

Graham pulled the car into a parking space. Out the windshield she could see her future for at least the next month. It looked barren for the moment, but as the sun cracked on the horizon, the bodies would make their way to deck. He spun the key, killing the engine and turned to her. "It's not about that, Jo. You know that no matter what, I got your back. I just don't think you truly understand how hard this is going to be."

"My dad has worked his fingers to the bone on that boat all these years for *me*. I'm not going to let the bank take his house now, when he needs it most."

"He makes a point about it not being your bill. If he was so worried about it, he should have paid it off."

"Do you have any clue how much his hospital bills have added up to this last year?"

Reaching down, Graham took her wrist. "I know how proud you are. How you don't want to take a loan from me or Keller, but I don't want you to get hurt or killed when it doesn't have to be this way."

"You're being melodramatic!"

"I'm not. I swear. This job is life and death every minute of every day."

"I don't have any other choice. I have to trust that I'm strong enough to do this."

He released her hand and turned away, looking out the window and biting on his upper lip. No doubt he was searching his mind for another argument. When none came, he slipped out of the car and started down the dock.

CHAPTER FOUR

Keller stepped up onto the deck just in time to see Jo jump on board from the dock. Her long hair that swayed back and forth at her hips last night was now twisted up and tucked under a hat. She wore an old blue flannel jacket that he recognized as her father's over a big turtle neck and her jeans. Her short legs might have tripped her up, but instead she landed graceful, with a slight bend at the knee, and didn't even look haggard by their contest from the evening before.

He tipped his wrist to check his watch and then sipped the coffee from the large clay mug. "You're late."

"Sorry, Captain." Graham said.

Smart man.

Keller didn't accept excuses on a standard day, and with a woman on board his fishing vessel, today was anything but normal. "It's okay," he mumbled as he pointed to the large stack of iron cages at the end of the deck and the rest of the crew gathering. "Let's start checking pots and making sure they're ready to fish. Jolanda, I need to talk to you."

He tossed his head, directing back down toward the cabin door. Following her into the galley, his mind wandered back to the night before, the tight knit pants and large sweater showed off her small waist and the curve of her hips. And all that hair. Before last night he usually saw her dressed more like she was now. Even when they ran into each other at the cannery, jeans and a sweatshirt appeared to be her uniform.

Last night he'd tried to write off his new-found attraction as a hallucination of closing time, but in the harsh light and even with a hangover, he was still seeing her in a new, softer light.

In the galley, he waved his hand toward the table, but wasn't surprised when she firmly planted her feet and crossed her arms in front of her chest. She'd proven the night before that she wasn't about to bow down to the will of any man.

But this wasn't last night. "This is my boat, and I'm the captain here."

"So?"

So? That meant he got what he wanted, no questions asked. "I don't think you understand the chain of command. If you're going to be on my crew—"

"You didn't bring me down here to try and talk me out of this?"

His stomach heaved as if they were already on the open sea. She'd seen through him. "I'm not against you, but I don't think you understand that I'm teetering on the edge here."

She twisted away, shaking her head. "I should have known you'd go back on your word."

He held up his hand and stepped closer to her. "Can you listen to me for one minute before you push this issue? I want you to know what it could cost me and the rest of my guys."

She nodded once, but still stood defiant.

"It hasn't been easy since my dad's heart attack. I know all about fishing, but not so much about running a business."

Her shoulders dropped and her gaze fell. "I'm sorry about your father."

"I'm not looking for sympathy."

"Did you resent having to come back?"

Was she talking about Brie? Did everyone know about his messed-up love life? "I didn't have a choice. Someone had to step up and run the company and I'm the oldest son. But, I'm barely keeping my head above water."

"I'm not asking you for a handout. I want to earn my way."

Keller pointed out toward the deck. "That's all those guys up-top want too. Last year they made thirty percent less than the year before. Now, Fred tells me some of them are talking about finding another boat because they're afraid that I'm cursing our whole damn season."

"Do you realize how stupid you sound?"

"Yes. I know you and most other people think superstition is absurd. I do too, but my crew believes in it. I can't bring in my quota without a crew."

"I'm not trying to screw you. If I knew of another way to make the money I need, I wouldn't be bothering you." She took a step back from him and leaned against the wall. Her shoulders slumped from the load she was carrying.

In some ways, he felt like he was looking in a mirror. "You'd only make money, if I make my quota. I can't do that without a strong, unified crew."

"My father always talks so highly of you and your family. He told me the crew had their doubts when you and Reese took over, but he stayed loyal to you. Doesn't that stand for anything?" She pushed her way past him and started for the steps.

The part of him that realized she was giving up the fight should have been rejoicing, but the truth was, her words cut deep. Against better judgment, he reached out and grabbed her arm. "I want to do what's right and keep my word to you, but it's not only my family on the line."

She spun back and leveled her rich, brown eyes on him. "The only family I give a rat's ass about right now is mine."

How selfish!

But he understood it, admired it even. "Let's work out some kind of loan." Why did he keep offering her money he couldn't afford to lend? Was it because of those beautiful eyes?

"So, I'm indebted to you instead of the bank. As far as I can see, the bank has more honor than you."

"That's not fair!"

"None of it is."

"What will you do?"

"I don't know. You were my last hope."

He released her grip and watched her arm fall back to her side. With her shoulders slumped; she could disappear in the excess of her oversized clothes. Meek. Tiny. Frail. All the reasons she'd be a hazard on his boat. Too much was on the line for him to take a risk. Just like her, he had to put his family above everything else. "I'm sorry, Jo."

He braced himself for the fury, but instead a rogue wave of despair washed over her face and pulled her shoulders further down. Had this last disappointment broken her spirit? He hoped not. She didn't yell, didn't even say a single word. Just turned and walked away.

Keller paused and then followed her, hoping he could get her to understand. And forgive him. He hit the deck just in time to watch her make the jump to the dock. Once on solid ground she took off at top speed across the parking lot.

"Where's she going?"

That was Graham's voice sounding from behind him. Keller met his deckhand's glare. "It was a dumb idea and I was an idiot for playing along with her last night. We all know this is too dangerous. She can't do it."

"What, so you're going back on your word?" Norm argued. Of course he would see it that way. He was the oldest of the deckhands now that Lark was gone. From the same generation as his father.

His father. What would he say about Keller breaking his word? He tried to shake it off. What choice did he have? Besides, he hadn't really told her no. "I just explained the facts, how the job was too hard. *She* decided to walk away."

"I don't believe that," Graham challenged. "She was way too determined on the way over here."

"Determination and a buck fifty will get you a cup of coffee at the diner," Pete chastised. "Keller did the right thing, and you know it."

"When is it ever right to go back on your word?" Norm asked.

The squabbling amongst his men only increased the tension and Keller's anxiety. He'd tried to do the right thing for them, and now they were more restless than they'd been last night. "Nice. Six hours ago you say you'll jump boats before working with a woman. Now, you're angry that I let her go. Is there no pleasing you?"

Graham redirected his surprise to Norm. "Did you really do that? She's Lark's daughter, you know. Do you know what's going to happen to them if she can't make the money she needs?"

"I never said I'd jump," Norm said.

Pete barely waited for Norm to finish before he pitched in his two cents. "*I* did! And quit trying to be all noble, Graham. You weren't any happier than the rest of us about having a girl on deck, even if she is *your* girl."

Graham didn't even acknowledge the needling. Instead, he leveled his gaze on Keller. "Didn't your dad always say that a man is only as good as his word?"

What the hell was wrong with these people? Couldn't he make a single one of them happy?

Don't hire the girl. Don't break your word.

"To hell with you all! If you want to make money, you better get this boat ready to fish."

Turning his back on the crew and starting for the dock brought back all the same emotions from two years earlier. He'd been an ass the day he told his father he was giving up fishing for Brie, fourteen days before the massive heart attack that took his life.

The doctor said it'd been inevitable. Years and years of bad diet and sitting in the captain's chair had caught up with the ol' man, but Keller should have been there with him when it happened. It was a son's place.

His mother would say Brie was wrong to walk away from him, that good people stood by the ones they loved. Was he any better than Brie? He'd just turned his back on one of his crewman's family members.

How could he think he was strong enough to be the kind of captain this boat needed? The only one in the whole mix who seemed to have the guts to get the job done was Jo.

And he'd kicked her off the boat.

CHAPTER FIVE

Jo let the door close behind her as she followed her father into the house. He shuffled, giving most of his weight to the cane.

Frustration knotted her stomach, but she knew Lark had been even more disappointed than she had by his prognosis, so she carefully chose her words. "You heard the doctor, you need to pick up your foot and try not to drag it."

"That little boy doesn't know what he's talking about."

Jo shifted the shopping bags in her arms. The "little boy" was the new doctor at Iliukiuk Family and Health Services, David Sutherland. He was old enough to have graduated medical school and fulfilled his residency.

"If you don't listen to what he says, you're going to lose your foot. Or did you miss that part?"

Her hopes for good news from Sutherland, had been dashed when she found out her father had been hiding a large ulcer on his right foot. The infection and a stash of ginger snaps she'd found hidden behind the cans of soup in the pantry explained why she couldn't keep his blood sugar in line.

At least her hangover had faded after eating lunch at the diner, a treat from her father who was thrilled that Keller had shown his jellyfish spine and broken his word.

"I'd like to see them try and take my foot."

She ignored his bravado and continued as if she hadn't heard it. "Sit down in that chair and take off your sock and shoe while I go make the Epsom salt bath."

Lark dropped down to the large recliner and then checked his watch. The fourth time he'd done so in the last fifteen minutes.

"Are you late for a date?" She called out over her shoulder but didn't wait for an answer. Instead she went about the task, turning on the water in the kitchen sink and letting it run to get hot. Finding the old dishpan and washing it with bleach water before filling it with the prescribed mixture; she tried to push her worries aside.

"What do you want for dinner?" Jo asked as she sat on the old footstool in front of her father and set the pan on the floor.

"I want to see you stop worrying and smile like you used to." His voice was meek, and the lines of his face soft as he moved his foot into the water, careful not to splash.

She dropped her stare trying to avoid his face. The weight of her guilt over his failing health was enough to bear without adding his concerns to her conscious. "How can I not worry?"

"I've been thinking. We should just move into an apartment. I see in the paper that there's one over the grocery store. I can afford it on my social security."

"I'm not moving into that dump, not when we have this house. I can work and pay for the loan."

"You shouldn't have to work that hard, and someday soon Graham is going to offer you up a ring. You're going to make a home with him."

She suppressed the scream bubbling up in her gut. "Graham and I are just friends. And you know that."

"The best relationships are built on friendship. Lust and romance fade. Look at your Mom and me. Graham's a good man. He'll treat you right and take care of you."

He's a fisherman. He'd never be home.

"We don't feel that way about each other. You should see the types of girls he dates."

Her father laughed. "Just sowing oats."

Lark was probably right on that point, but it didn't validate the other. "He's just my friend. I guess I'll go to the bank tomorrow after work and try to talk them into refinancing the balance of the loan."

He lowered his chin and found a spot in the worn carpet to examine.

"What are you not telling me?"

"They've turned me down for that already."

"What? When? Why?"

"The hospital bills from last summer. They were so much. I've missed the last two payments on the house. They won't refinance unless I make the loan current— and there's just no way."

"How much?"

"I just thought if I could get this damn foot healed and get back on the boat, I'd have the money before they tried to foreclose."

"*What* is the balance?"

"Too much!"

Her patience was wearing thin, and she'd had enough of his avoidance game. "Just tell me, damn it!"

"Three thousand dollars to bring the loan current."

"And fifteen thousand more to pay it off completely?"

He nodded.

"Shit!"

"That's no way for a lady to talk!"

She pushed her fingers through her hair and rubbed her temples. Ladies who spoke the way her father expected her to probably didn't have to carry the weight of the world. Jo tried to force her anger aside. Lark never intended to get sick, always thought he would have this coming season to make the money to pay off the loan.

He didn't want her to take on his responsibilities either, but he should know she couldn't walk away. "I don't have any other choice. I have to get Keller to man up and let me go out."

"No! I know you don't see it now, but he did the right thing."

Jo wasn't about to bow down and let chivalry or chauvinism keep her from doing what had to be done, but arguing about it with her father wasn't going to change his opinion and this building anger looming between them was taking a heavy toll.

She stood and leaned in to hug his neck. "I'm not going to let the bank take the house, Daddy."

His large arms wrapped around her shoulders and he patted her back. "It's just a building. Your safety is what matters most to me. Home is where you and I are together."

"I love you, too." She kissed his temple and held on to him longer than normal. His words meant a lot. She knew that Lark lived behind the tough armor he always wore. The house was small, but it had been theirs. He'd done his best to make it home for her after his divorce, and to lose it would hurt him a lot more than he was letting on.

She pulled back. "I'm going to start some dinner. Leave your foot in the water for a few more minutes and then I'll bandage it for you."

She wasn't even half way to the kitchen when a heavy knock reversed her direction.

Maybe Keller came to his senses.

Now, that was just stupid. As tough as those fishermen all talked, when it came to bucking tradition or doing the hard thing, they shivered in their boots.

Please don't be Graham offering another handout.

Looking through the window and seeing her mother's face made her want to go back and recant her last thought. She'd gladly deal with Graham or Keller instead. At least she had a way of making them see her side of things.

Knowing there was no other option, she opened the door and her arms to her mother. "What in the world are you doing here?"

"Your father called me this morning." Elle pulled back from the embrace, and looked around the living room from the safety of the old covered porch.

Lark twisted in the chair. He appeared to be trying to get a better look at his ex-wife. "Now that you're here, don't stand out in the cold. Come in."

Her mother hesitated, then spoke to Jo. "I was hoping maybe you and I could go somewhere else and talk."

Lark responded before Jo could. "You're being ridiculous. No one's going to bite. Get in out of the cold."

Jo's gut twisted again. She recognized the look on her mother's face. It broadcasted, *If I step into Lark's presence, I'll fall back under his spell.* Funny, when her parents were still together she'd never noticed the tension between them, but her mom's unwillingness to have anything to do with her ex, even if it benefited Jo, had always put her in the tenuous middle.

"It's up to you, Mom. We can go somewhere else if you want."

The sound of the water sloshing around told Jo that her father was trying to get up, most likely to restate his wants and desires. "She just spent seven hours on a plane, she should come in—"

"Sit down! Please!" Jo turned to him. "You have to listen to the doctor." When he continued to push against the cane Jo covered her face with her hands and turned from him. "Why can't you just follow orders so I can have one less thing to worry about?"

Her mother's arm looped through hers and the other came around her shoulder. A patient whisper hit her ear. "Okay, Jo. You've had enough. Where are the bandages for your father?"

Jo pressed her finger tips to her eyes. "It's not your responsibility. I'll do it in a minute."

"No, you won't. I'm a nurse. Remember? I'm going to take care of your father's foot and you're going to go down to the diner and take a break. I'll meet you there when I'm done, and we'll talk."

As she reached for her coat hanging on the hook, Jo knew fleeing was wrong, even if her mother had offered, but she couldn't bring herself to stay. Having to deal with the two of them in the same room was the last push that would send her tumbling off the precipice of sanity. "Make it the Elbow Room."

CHAPTER SIX

A shot had sounded like a perfect idea when Keller had stormed into the Elbow Room after the fight with his crew, but when he sat at the bar, all he could see was Jolanda's dark brooding eyes, and all he could hear was her pleas.

The remnant of his hangover throbbed in his temples, reminding him there was a penance to pay if he crawled inside a bottle. He had a real problem to solve and needed a clear head, so he ordered the black coffee.

With the tip of his finger, Keller circled the rim of the coffee mug. The Elbow Room normally crawled with guys who'd do anything to get their chance on a crab boat. Finding a warm body to fill the gaping hole in his crew wouldn't be too hard if his guilty conscience would let him consider anyone but Jo.

He rolled the phone in his hand and pushed the buttons that brought up his contact book, scrolling down to his brother's name. Reese knew the job and was good at it. The baby wasn't due for five weeks. The fishing gods willing, Keller could have him home safe in plenty of time for his kid's birth.

But if Reese was still at sea when the baby came, would his wife ever forgive either of them?

"Jo! I thought you were off tonight."

Keller looked up into the bartender's face and his wide smile. Good to know that Keller wasn't the only one who reacted to her like that. Still he couldn't bring himself to face her. Not after the argument on the boat.

"I'm not here to pour 'em, Ralph, I'm here to drink 'em. I'll have a draft, please."

By the sound of the bar stool scraping against the gritty hardwood, she was just a few stools to his left.

Her voice sounded cheerful, but he could sense that layer of exhaustion he'd seen in her eyes that morning. "Can I put in for an order of the crab nachos too?"

Keller picked up his cup and sipped. The coffee was cold and seemed heavier, bitterer than it had a few moments ago. Because of his guilt?

He heard the heavy glass sliding against the mahogany. Her barstool rattled as she slid off, but he kept his gaze on the drink. One look in her eyes and the façade that had allowed him to dismiss honor would crumble.

"Is it that easy for you to ignore me now?"

Easy?

He lifted his chin and glanced in her direction. "I didn't hear you come in." How did the lie slip by his lips so effortlessly?

Her chest heaved slightly and a grin pushed up her cheeks. Great. She didn't believe him. She leaned back against the bar, close enough to him he could smell the fruity perfume she wore. Or was that her shampoo? Her long hair was now freed from the clips and the hat she wore earlier. She'd pulled it over the shoulder closest to him. "So which one of these yokels did you hire?"

"Nobody yet."

"What are you waiting for? I figured you'd pull out by the end of the week."

What could he say? The weight of the phone in his hand gave him a thought. "I have a call into Reese. I'm hoping he'll come up."

"I didn't know that was an option. I mean when I heard he wasn't captaining the *Melbourne*, I assumed he'd given up fishing."

He shook his head. "Can't believe everything this rumor mill spits out. His wife's expecting. He wanted to take some time off to be with her and the baby." Yeah, *some time*, like the rest of his life.

"Reese is going to be a daddy?" Her laugh sounded almost musical. "That's wonderful. He'll be such a good father."

That grabbed Keller's attention. "How do you know that?"

She shrugged her shoulders. "Maybe I don't. But, you sort of get to know the guys who come into the cannery. He always seemed kind-hearted."

His brother was that. And if Keller asked, Reese would answer his call.

"Don't you think it's unfair to ask him to miss the birth of his first child? But then, I guess you don't care too much about those kinds of things?"

Though he'd seen and interacted with Jo before, it wasn't until last night that he'd felt he got to know her at all. "Why would you say that?"

"This is a small town. And maybe you guys think you breeze in and out without making a mark on us locals, but when you get drunk in here you talk. And what you say to one person becomes common knowledge along the gossip chains."

"I want my brother to be home when his child comes."

"But not more than you want to fill your boat on your terms."

"No. Family comes first."

"Since when?"

Since his father died with no one from his family around him, but he couldn't say that. "Let's just say I learned that lesson the hard way. Okay?"

"Is that why Brie left you?"

How did she know about that? Yeah. Right. Gossip chains.

"That's none of your business."

"Oh. I touched a nerve."

"I'm not having this discussion with you." He motioned to the bartender. This time he ordered the whiskey he'd held at bay earlier.

"Watch it, Kell. Don't get drunk again and make promises you're not willing to keep."

At her prodding, the guilt bubbled into acidic anger, pressing against the back of his throat and giving him the worse heartburn he'd experienced in a long time.

"Your nachos are up, Jo," Ralph said.

"Thanks. I'm going to take them over to the booth."

As she crossed the bar, Keller could feel her presence pull away from him. He hadn't felt such a connection to anyone in a long time. Not since Brie. But Jo was different. She stood tall. Pushed buttons. Made him look in the mirror and examine who he was.

He picked up the shot and took a small sip, just enough to quiet the whispers of guilt. How dare she even *think* she knew what went on between him and his former fiancée? How dare she be right?

* * * *

Jo slipped into the booth and took a bite of the nachos, then followed it with a gulp of the beer. Neither the food nor the drink could settle her nauseous stomach.

What in the world had she been thinking?

When she saw Keller at the bar, she'd thought she'd try to guilt him into changing his mind. Instead, she'd pissed him off. She was on a real roll lately. Everyone she knew was angry at her.

"Jo. Jo. Jo."

She didn't have to look up to know it was her mother. The way she repeated her name in the exhale of a long breath told her disappointment. "Just sit down."

After tossing her purse and coat into the corner, Elle loosened her scarf, releasing her blond hair. "I'm not going to mince words with you. Okay? You know how I feel about all of this."

She did, and this push-pull between her parents was the last thing she needed. "I can't just leave him. He's my father."

"I know that and I've always done my best not to interfere with your relationship with him, especially when you were young. But you're not a child anymore, you're a grown woman and it's not right that he holds you down here."

"What are you talking about?"

Elle picked up the grease-stained menu from behind the salt and pepper shaker, but only glanced at it before returning it and grabbing a handful of napkins to wipe her hands. "His bills are not your responsibility."

Jo slid her plate of nachos toward her mother. Elle waved them off. "He's not asking me to pay them. He says the same things you are saying, but I don't want to see him lose the house. *I* don't want to lose that house."

"He just told me he's going to get an apartment for the two of you. But, you're old enough to be on your own. You should be going to college, not working in that cannery."

Jo's temples throbbed again, and she let her eyes flutter close. "Not everyone is college material."

"But *you* are. You are far too bright to be stuck here."

"My family's here."

"What am I? What about Allen? And your brother and sister. We're your family too."

She couldn't meet her mother's eyes. Instead, she reached for the mug and drank long. What should have gotten better when she became an adult had been escalating since she graduated. Once her court-mandated split visitation had lifted, she'd spent a lot less time with her mother and that side of the family. She felt guilty about that, but felt guiltier when she got on a plane and left her dad home alone. "All of you have each other. Who does Dad have besides me?"

"You can't give up your life to take care of him."

"If you were the one who was sick, I'd be there for you. It's what I should do as a daughter, take care of my parents."

"Would you? Would you be there for me? Or would you say that I have Allen and my other kids?"

Jo slid her hand across the table, searching out her mom's, but not looking up. "If you need me, I'm there for you. Right now, Dad needs me to be here."

Her mother gripped Jo's offered hand. "The kids miss you like crazy. Do you know how much you upset them when you stormed out last week saying you weren't ever coming back?"

"I shouldn't have said that in front of them." Her temper was her downfall, and she regretted not making things right with her siblings. "How did Allen's trip go?"

"I'll get to that in a minute. First, I want to finish this fight from last week. I want you to know something. When I told Allen about it, he told me to give you the money."

Her ears perked up and she met her mother's gaze for the first time. What she saw squashed her hopes. "You can't give Dad your husband's money."

She shook her head. "It's *our* money and if it was for you, I would write the check in a heartbeat. But it's not for you, it's for him."

"It's my house."

"It's *his* house. It's a mortgage he's had since our divorce. It's a balloon payment that he's known about for twenty years and should have planned for."

"He did. But then there were the hospital bills."

"If not that, it would have been something else. He's a fisherman. They all think the same way. Live for today, catch more fish tomorrow. He's never believed money was for saving. He always spent it as fast as he made it."

"Is that why you divorced him?" Part of her found it funny that in twenty years this was the first time she'd felt strong enough to ask her mother that question. Before now, she'd always guessed at why her mom had packed them up and taken off for Fairbanks, leaving her Dad behind.

When her father came home and found them gone, he'd fought for—and won—split custody of her, beginning the cycle of long trips back and forth between Fairbanks and the islands.

"It was a factor, but only part of it. I didn't get married to be alone. Another reason is what I saw in that house tonight. The way he tries to control you—he did that to me, too."

"But he doesn't."

"You don't see it because he's a master at it. He lays out this heavy blanket of guilt saying that his whole world revolves around you, but it's not true. In his mind, he's the center of his own universe and he does what it takes to keep his possessions locked up and close to him."

"It's not true!" With every accusation, Jo's anger raised another notch. When Elle attacked Lark, Jo couldn't help but believe her mother was attacking her too. "That's my father you're belittling."

"If it wasn't true, he wouldn't have talked you out of going to college. He wouldn't have convinced you that you didn't want it."

Jo might have argued, but she was tired of it. She'd been excited at the prospect of going to college but felt bad about leaving her dad behind. Lark hadn't influenced her decision, but her mother blamed him nonetheless.

"Allen was offered the job."

Another heavy brick fell atop the load of hardships she was already carrying. "You're moving to Oregon?"

"Not unless you're okay with it."

Jo wrapped her arms around herself, protecting herself from further pain. "Who am I to tell you what to do?"

"You are my daughter. I love you. I don't want you to feel like I deserted you."

"It's hardly any different. It's a plane ride whether I visit you in Fairbanks or I visit you in Portland."

"That's true, but it feels different. I feel like leaving the state is like crossing some boundary. I can't explain how it made me feel when you stormed out last weekend. I've always hated the distance between us. I always wanted you with me, all the time, but I knew you needed your dad too. I didn't want to be selfish."

Again she felt as though her mother twisted the truth. Would Elle have given her access to Lark if a judge hadn't ordered it? Jo doubted it, and pulled her hand away. She couldn't stand in the way of her mother's happiness any more than she could abandon her father. "It's okay. You and Allen should do what's best for you and your kids."

Elle reached across the table, gripping Jo's wrist again. "*You* are one of my kids!"

"I know, but I'm an adult with my own life."

"Will you visit?"

"Of course." Inside, Jo chuckled. She felt like the walls were closing in on her. First she had to come up with the money to bail her dad out, and then she would have to find even more money to visit her family in the lower forty-eight.

"Would you consider coming with us? Allen's job at the university would mean reduced tuition for you."

"It's a medical school. I never wanted—"

"They have affiliates you could go to."

College. A normal life. Her mom and siblings close. As bad as she wanted it all, it was just a pipe dream. "Not now. I can't leave Dad when he's so sick."

"If he would listen to his doctors and control his diet, things would be better for him." She pulled a pen out of her purse, scribbling a name and number on a napkin. "I want you to call this woman. She's a friend of mine. We were nurses together when I was married to your dad. She's retired now but can come and take care of your dad's foot and monitor his blood sugar."

"*I* can do that."

"I know you can, but you have this father-daughter pull between you. He doesn't listen to you, wants to be in charge. This woman can be the bad guy and take that stress out of your relationship with him."

"I'm sure she's not cheap."

"Your father qualifies for medical assistance. She has all the paperwork he needs to fill out. There might be a co-pay, but it'll be small."

Jo crumpled up the napkin and pushed it into the pocket of her sweat jacket. "I'll think about it."

Her mother pushed herself out of the booth. "Come here, give me a hug. I have to go."

Jo dragged herself to the end of the bench and stood. "Leave? You just got here."

"My plane leaves in less than an hour."

"So, you're going to spend fourteen hours round trip on a plane, to spend less than one with me?"

Elle reached out and pulled Jo into a hug. "I'd go to the ends of the earth for you. You've got to know that." She paused and released Jo from her grip. "Your dad called me down here to talk you out of going out on that fishing boat, but that's not why I came. I don't like the idea. It's dangerous, but I trust you and I believe in you."

"Keller backed out."

"Your dad told me that, too."

She pushed a stray strand of her hair back over her ear. "Do you really think I could do it?"

"I know that you can do whatever you set your heart on."

Jo wrapped her arms around her mother's neck and held on, wondering how much time would pass before she got the chance to hug her again.

She still felt the need to help her father and care for him, it'd never be right to walk away, but her mother had a point too. She did have the strength to pursue her goals. And she'd survive on the deck of the *Sydney*. She had everything it would take. All she had to do was convince Keller of that.

Her mother kissed her cheek, and then tugged on a strand of her hair. "Take care of yourself. And think about coming to Portland with us."

"I'll think about it. After Dad's doing better."

With her mom gone, her gaze drifted back to the bar. Keller still sat on his stool. Now, his cell phone was glued to his ear. Was Reese hopping a plane, taking the slot on deck she'd already earned?

Like hell!

She stomped across the bar, and put her hand on his forearm, just as he pushed a button on the phone.

"I earned that spot on your crew, and it's not fair for you to give it to someone else, even if it *is* your brother."

He twisted the heel of his boot into the floor as he pivoted to her. His teeth clenched. "Earned? What did you do to earn it? Drink more whiskey than me? Do you really think that prepares you for what goes on out there?"

"You don't even have a clue how strong I am. You'd rather pull your brother away from his family—"

"Damn it!" Keller tossed his phone to the bar and turned away from her. Picking up the shot glass, he tossed the amber liquid back.

His anger sent her stumbling back a step. "What's wrong?"

"Reese can't come."

"I can do it."

He turned away from her and she noticed his hand gripping the bar and a tremble in his biceps.

"Kell? There's something more going on, isn't there?"

He slid his empty glass toward the back of the bar. "That was my mother on the phone. They're all at the hospital. Carol went into labor."

"I thought you said she wasn't due until December."

"She's not. She might be losing the baby. I should go home. I need to go home." He stood up and turned quickly, running right in to her.

She wrapped her arms around him, holding him up, but pulling him close. "I'm sorry. I really am."

Though hugging him had been about offering comfort at first, the feel of his body next to hers sated an urge that had been pulsing inside her since the night before. She brushed her cheek to his broad shoulder and was overwhelmed with the scent of salt water and stale cigarette smoke.

Funny how it comforted her, reminded her of home.

Keller straightened and stood on his own. He gripped the side of the bar, and turned his head away from her. "It's really too soon to tell. Maybe the doctors can stop her labor or something."

"It's possible. You should stay positive and not worry about the worst case scenario."

He nodded. "But there's no way Reese will be able to come up and work."

Jo leaned in closer and lowered her voice. "Look, I know you have a lot on the line, but this is easy. You need one more deck hand and I need the job. Don't dismiss me without giving me a chance."

He let his gaze find hers, but then closed his eyes. She watched his chest go up and down with each breath, and she could almost see scales trying to balance in his mind.

"Okay," he whispered, "One trip, because you won the bet. From there, you have to prove yourself like everyone else."

"You won't regret this!"

He met her gaze again. "I sort-of...already do."

So much pain in his blue eyes, part of Jo felt guilty for pushing him into doing what he so obviously didn't want to. Even worse, she couldn't get Keller—or her desire to be close to him—out of her mind. Too bad, he didn't seem to feel the same way about her.

"Go get yourself a full set of gear in the morning and then report to the boat. I'll have Graham work with you so you can pass the coast guard inspection we have at three o'clock. We're leaving port at nine tomorrow night."

CHAPTER SEVEN

Jolanda knocked on the door to Mr. Crandell's office, even though it was open. His balding head was buried in a ledger and his fingers tapped away on an adding machine.

He was checking his employee's logs, as he did at the end of every day. Heaven help the poor sap who made a mistake. The tapping paused, but his eyes stayed down. "One moment, please."

And once again the clackity-clack resumed. She watched his left hand move down row by row in the ledger until he hit the bottom. He then picked up the red ink pen off the desk, made a small check mark on the column and looked up to her. "Jo! Please, come in. Have a seat."

She entered the office, suddenly intimidated by his large presence. Mr. Crandell might be a hard-ass—as most of the other employees referred to him—but if you did a good job, he was fair.

To her, he'd always been above board kind. Her books almost never had errors. "Thank you," she said as she dropped down to the old, wooden chair.

Like her boss, his office was simple and rugged. He'd understand her having to do what was best for her family. Wouldn't he?

"What can I help you with?"

"I need to take a leave of absence."

The warm smile he'd greeted her with flattened. "For how long? The crab fleet is heading out this week. We're going to be hitting our busiest time of the year."

"Well, you see, I picked up a job on the *Sydney*."

"Doing what?"

What do you think? "A deckhand."

"Who hired you?"

What is this, the Spanish inquisition? "Keller."

Mr. Crandell shook his head and clucked his tongue against the roof of his mouth. Jo couldn't decide who he was more disappointed in: her or Keller. "Ol' man Sveinsson, rest his soul, would never allow something like this."

"Then it's a good thing I didn't go to him for a job." The words were no sooner out and she regretted them.

Her boss looked at her as she'd just broken about a half-dozen commandments. Mr. Crandell was as old-school as many of these captains. He wouldn't find her off-the-cuff remarks funny. "What would your grandmother say if she heard you say such an awful thing, Miss Gilles?"

She certainly wouldn't approve. Jo could hear the old woman scolding her from beyond the grave. She gave a quick, half-nod to acknowledge his remark, but changed the subject back to the matter-at-hand. "Dad's medical bills are piling up and I need this job. It will only be for a few weeks. Can I have a leave or are you going to make me quit?"

He tossed the pen down to the desk and swiveled the chair around shifting his weight. "You know I don't like being backed into a corner. I've always treated you more than fair. If you were in a bind, I don't understand why you didn't come to me. If I give you a raise—"

"Sir, no disrespect, but I can't make what I need working for you."

Mr. Crandell's eyebrows knitted together, and his fingers tapped against the desk. Even though she'd prefaced the statement by deferring insolence, he'd taken it as a direct hit to his ego. "Well then, maybe you don't need this job at all."

"Don't fire me!" She tried hard to keep the pleading out of her voice. Her record should stand on its own. Besides, she'd spent enough time begging these last few days in order to get the job on the *Sydney*.

"If you want and like this job, you'll be at your desk bright and early with a shining face."

He was pushing her back to the wall, and her already knotted stomach twisted again. "I can't do that. If I don't show up at the boat tomorrow—"

"Well, it seems you have a tough decision to make. You can return some of the loyalty I've shown you over the years and not leave me shorthanded through the busiest time of the year, or you can put me in a bind, go fishing, and lose your place here."

Damn!

Jo really believed her past record would be enough to secure her job. She should have known if she wasn't being ever-faithful, the big dog would turn on her and bare his teeth. This was a small town with a big reputation based on the fishing industry, and this job was a good one. If she sacrificed it to get the house, she'd only be opening herself up to a new slew of problems when she got home. Standing, she picked up her purse from the floor. "You've given me something to think about."

He tipped his chin. "What's your answer?"

"I guess we'll both find out come nine tomorrow morning."

* * * *

Jo let herself into the house, and carefully closed the door, hoping not to wake her father. She twisted the lock behind her and hung her coat up on the hook. As she slipped her boots off, she heard the sound of his cane hitting the kitchen floor and noticed the light beneath the door.

Deciding on fight over flight, she walked toward the sound. "What are you still doing up?"

"I wasn't aware I had a bedtime. You've been with your mother this whole time?"

She shook her head as she took a seat at the table. "She's well on her way home by now. Keller was at the Elbow Room."

Lark took the seat across from her. "Doesn't surprise me."

"We had a long talk. He's going to let me go out."

He closed his eyes and she could see his Adam's apple bob as he swallowed hard. "I hate this."

"I wish you could have faith in me."

"Is that what you think this is about?" He reached across the table. "It's not about what I think you can or can't do. It's about what I don't want you to have to do."

She inched her hand toward him, wrapping her fingers around his. "It's important to me. You and this house are the two constants in my life. You've worked so hard for me, and I want to do this one thing for you."

"It's not right. You're risking too much. What about your job at the cannery?"

"After I talked to Keller, I went and saw Mr. Crandell. He fired me."

Lark's eyes shut. "That was a good job, one thing that's in short supply around here."

"I'll find another one after I pay off the house."

"I can live without this house. I would be perfectly happy in a small apartment, and as long as I know you're safe and happy."

She leaned back in the chair, crossing her arms in front of her chest. "Then what did you work all those years for?"

"For you! Don't you get that? It allowed me to take the time off to spend with you. It allowed me to have you for months on end. Don't get me wrong, I'm not happy about losing the house, but I'm more concerned about your safety than I am about this building. Please, don't do this."

She pushed herself to her feet, leaning against the table. "I've made up my mind, and I need you to respect that. Mom put me in touch with a woman who's going to come by here twice a day to help you with your foot and your medications. She's also going to bring some paperwork to get some help with the medical bills."

"I don't need anyone's help me. I'm fully capable—"

"But I'll feel better knowing she's coming and I'm meeting her first thing in the morning to pay her. So please, please, tell me you'll listen to her."

Lark's head dropped, and he stared at the worn linoleum. "When's the boat leaving?"

"Tomorrow night."

CHAPTER EIGHT

Keller crawled on the top of the stack, checking each bind securing the pots. Methodically, he moved: Left knee, left hand, right knee, right hand, inching his way back and forth. He pushed away his concern about what anyone watching him would think and focused on the job he felt most comfortable with.

He couldn't recall a single time his father did this chore. When Keller was a deck mate, it had always been his job. As a captain, he wanted to know it was as safe as possible; and the only way to be sure, was to do it himself.

Too many lives counted on it. Counted on him.

Maybe he was a better deck hand than captain.

Hearing Pete call his name, he turned to the deck and then followed the man's point to the dock. Lark approached, leaning heavily on a cane and showing the chinks in his armor. Something Keller had spent last season trying to ignore.

He scanned the deck for Jo. Not finding her, he surmised that she was still cleaning out the bait freezer with Graham. Hopping down, he dashed across the deck and jumped to the dock before Lark reached the boat and had to figure out how to cross with his injury.

Keller extended a hand to his recent employee. "Couldn't stay away, huh?"

Lark gave all his weight to the cane, gripping it with both hands. Keller suspected it was his way of avoiding the gesture. "This isn't a friendly visit, Mr. Sveinsson."

"Really?" Keller let the question hang in the air. This had to be about Jo.

"Man-to-man, don't take my baby girl out there."

"She's an adult. She makes her own mind."

"Hmf. You're telling me. But you see her. You know she can't do the work."

Keller slid his left foot back, shifting his weight and turning his eyes toward the bait freezer. Did he? "She's worked really hard around here today. You should be proud."

"Of course I'm proud, but I'm also a concerned father. I killed myself for your family all these years so my daughter wouldn't have to work hard. I never wanted her to take my worries on for herself."

Funny. With Lark focusing the microscope, Keller could see the parallels between his and Jo's life even more clearly. Whether parents believed it or not, when the time came, children became caregivers. He understood, probably better than most, why Jo couldn't turn her back on her father's problems. "I know that. But, you've raised her well. Maybe it's time to cut the strings and let her—"

"Kill herself? Or one of these guys who are like family to me? Geez, it hasn't been that long since you worked a deck. You know the havoc one bad hand can cause."

Lark didn't exaggerate; a small mistake could have deathly consequences. That fact had caused him to go back on his word once, but no more flip-flopping. This time, he planned to keep his word to Jo. "I've decided to give her the chance to sink or swim. It'd be nice if her father did the same, instead of dooming her to fail."

"Is that what you're trying to do, Dad?"

Shit.

Those words hadn't really been meant for Jo's ears.

Lark's focused gaze swept from Keller to Jo. "I want you to give up this fool notion and come home this minute."

The acid in Keller's stomach sloshed as if they were riding the high waves; but this was a family storm, and he was an invader. Then again, he'd been the one who agreed to let Jo fish. The least he could do was stand by her side and support her.

"Would you look at me, Dad? I'm not the little girl in pigtails you used to ship off to Mom's when you went out to fish?"

"No? You're behaving just like you used to every summer when you came home. Acting out to get my attention, forcing me to prove to you how much I love you. This boat and that sea is no place for a young girl."

"I thought we talked this out last night."

"I understand why you want to do this. But, then, I stared at the ceiling all night thinking about the danger."

"Lark," Keller hoped interrupting would diffuse the tension. "Give her some credit for trying to help."

"Stay out of this, Sveinsson. This is between me and my daughter."

"No, Dad. There is no more discussing it. Keller gave me this job, and I'm taking it. All I'm asking from you is to give me a few weeks to take care of business. That's it."

Lark's hands tightened around the curved handle of the cane. Keller noticed his arms begin to tremble. "Jo.

Why don't you take your dad home? I'm going to send the rest of the crew on to dinner anyway. Just be back in time to push off."

Jo slowly exhaled a deep breath. "Okay. Thanks."

As he watched the two walk down the dock, he couldn't help but notice the uncomfortable tension between them, tempered with love and concern. It reminded him of his own father, the way they'd butted heads and the way they were always there for the other.

Except for when Hal had needed him most.

He and his father had fought in a similar way just before Hal set course on his last trip—only in reverse. His father had pleaded for just one more season and Keller refused. He'd put his foot down for independence much the way Jo just had, and lived to regret it.

Keller shook off the painful memories and took the stairs to the wheelhouse two at a time, letting the door slam behind him. He picked up the clipboard. Scanning down his to-do list, he checked off the completed items one by one.

He heard the heater kick on and the warmth penetrated through the layers of clothes. Peeling off his coat, and sitting in the pilot chair, he continued to scan the page.

All that was left was to fuel the boat on the way out, and they had an appointment for that in a few hours.

He picked up the microphone for the outdoor speaker and directed, "Go grab yourself some dinner guys. Just get your asses back here by nine o'clock. We're leaving whether you're here or not."

He hung the mike up on the hook, and turned away from the deck. His mind wandered back to Jo, and he couldn't help but wonder if taking her out was the right thing. Lark was so angry and rightfully concerned, but she was the most tenacious woman he'd ever met.

Under all the large layered clothing and bitter outer shell, she was stunning and tender. The kind of woman he always thought it would take to put up with a man like him.

A woman not unlike his mother. She had spent her whole married life catering to his father, who spent more days at sea than on dry land, and never once complained. They had made their marriage work, though Keller never understood how.

The ring of the satellite phone drew his attention. A check of the caller ID confirmed it was his brother calling.

With one simple hello, he could hear the pain in Reese's voice. He knew protocol. If he was calling hours before the boat was to ship out, there was trouble.

Keller bit his thumb nail, and dug deep for a calm voice. "What's going on?"

"The doctors were able to stall Carol's labor."

The pressure in Keller's chest eased, and he took a full breath. "That's wonderful."

"I wouldn't go that far. All is good for the moment, but the little one could change his mind and try again at any moment."

"You have to hold on to hope, Reese. The doctors know what they're doing."

"We're trying, but it's scary. Everyone at the hospital is taking it minute by minute."

Keller had buried his father and had his heart broken in the last eighteen months. Both events had left scars so deep he wasn't sure he would stop hurting from either.

But, he couldn't even begin to put himself in his brother's shoes. "Is there anything I can do to help?"

"I wish. I wish there was something I could do. You know? I don't like feeling this helpless."

That was something the brothers had in common. Keller hated being too far away to even lend a hug. "Anything you need. I'm a phone call away. Promise me you'll give me regular updates."

His brother choked out his thanks before the line went dead in Keller's ear. He dropped the handset into the base and the reality of the situation sunk in.

If Reese called, he'd always answer. There was no doubt about that. But, if he couldn't fish this season, the Sveinsson Corporation would have to close. All of their employees would be added to the largely unemployed population. The legacy his father had spent his whole life building for his sons would be lost. Burnt to the ground by the choices he'd made.

Not able to think about worst case scenario anymore, Keller picked up the phone and dialed. "Have you been able to find anything out yet?" he asked when his mother answered.

"I've spent all day on the phone wheeling and dealing. I picked up some, about thirty thousand pounds."

Keller tried to do the math in his head, but stumbled over the numbers and began scribbling on the yellow pad by the phone. "Thanks, Mom. I owe you one."

"I just hope you're still saying that at the end of the season."

CHAPTER NINE

"I hope you dickweeds brought money." Pete came into the galley, shuffling a deck of cards as he walked. "Because I don't take no Visa card."

Graham, Fred, and Norm all slipped in to the booth, while Jo leaned back against the refrigerator and tried to just blend into the surroundings. She didn't want to play poker or throw around insults with these guys.

At one time or another, she'd dealt with all of them individually, whether it was at the cannery or the Elbow Room. In a group like this, it seemed their IQs dropped twenty points. Each one felt they had to be more badass than the others.

What she wanted was to go up and really talk to Keller and find out why he'd come to her defense with her father.

But, the wheelhouse was the captain's domain, and she'd pushed Keller far enough today. If she dared to ignore the sanctity of his space or challenge the chain of command, she'd be buying trouble.

The last thing she needed.

"How long before we get to the fishing grounds, Graham?" Even though she'd been careful to focus her question to just one, the other three chuckled and murmured.

Graham picked up the dealt cards off the table. "About eighteen to twenty hours, I guess."

Pete reordered the cards in his hand. "Yeah, plenty of time for you to make the men-folk some coffee, sweet-cheeks."

Jo took a step away from the galley wall, and stood up straight. "Yeah, plenty of time for you to kiss my ass."

Till now, ignoring Pete's crass, mostly inappropriate language hadn't been all that hard. She'd encountered his type day in and day out in the cannery. And her father was one of them after all. They worked hard and showed the world an unbreakable shell. Mostly an act of bravado. Jo understood that, and most days she could ignore it, but she drew the line at being degraded.

"Jo!" Graham shot her a disapproving glare. He'd warned her that the crew would share the cooking responsibilities on the boat, and Keller had made it clear that every greenhorn gets pushed around. She'd been advised to expect nothing different than a good, old-fashioned hazing.

She'd take whatever they threw at her, but she wouldn't do so lying down.

"Was that an offer, sweetie?" Pete countered.

Jo pushed her flannel shirt off her shoulders, exposing the thin, white tank top underneath and leaned against the table. Her arms were taunt, and she shook her head, letting her hair fall forward. She pursed her lips, doing her best Marilyn Monroe impersonation—if Marilyn had dark hair and skin. "Sorry, Pete, I don't think you're man enough for a woman like me."

He lunged to his feet, but Fred grabbed his arm, pulling him back. "Let's just play cards. Leave Jo alone."

Pete adjusted himself in the seat, and picked his cards up off the table. "You're right, Fred, she's not worth my time."

Fred might have been willing to pull back his friend-the-caveman, but he wasn't about to let Jo completely off the hook. "Since you've decided not to play. It would be nice if you made coffee for everyone."

Jo drew in a sharp breath and opened her mouth to tell Fred exactly what she thought he could do with his idea and the coffee pot, when Graham interrupted. "It would be awful nice of you."

Taking the hint—that was about as subtle as a wooden club to the head—Jo swallowed the anger and started the requested task. It had been stupid to think they'd save the hazing for the deck.

Ten minutes later, the coffee was done and her anger had dialed back to a low simmer. She set cups in front of Graham, Norm, and Fred who muttered their thanks, but didn't divert their attention from the game. She picked up Pete's from the counter, and was twisting back when he chose to needle her one more time.

"You know what would go really great with this coffee: a cake. Why don't you bake us one, sweetheart?"

If Pete could have held his tongue just a few seconds longer the cup would have been resting on the table, but he didn't and before she could stop herself, she'd tipped her hand and dumped its contents into his lap.

Pete jumped to his feet, gripping the pants and pulling them away from his skin. "What the hell is wrong with you?"

"With *me*? You pig!" Jo lunged forward, though she wasn't sure what effect it would have against a guy who had six inches and at least a hundred pounds on her. Arms came around her waist, pulling her back and lifting her off the ground. She didn't have to look back to know it was Graham. There wasn't another soul on this boat who'd protect her from herself.

"Knock it off!" His voice came louder than the mottled murmurs of the other guys.

"Don't tell me! Tell that asshole." She squirmed against Graham's restraints.

Pete pulled free of Norm's hold, landing in front of her.

"What did you expect, honey-cakes? Did you really think you were out here to fish with the men? Get used to the galley. It's all you're going to be seeing for the next few weeks."

Fred moved between the two of them. As Graham stepped back, Fred pushed Pete in the opposite direction. "You know damn well that's not the way it's going to happen. Keller hired her as a deckhand."

"Put me down!" Jo screeched, fighting against Graham's hold. The boat hurled forward and to the left throwing her and Graham against the refrigerator. Fred grabbed the table as Pete fell back on his butt.

She heard a thunderous explosion of Keller's steps descending from the wheelhouse and realized he'd thrown the boat into neutral.

"What the hell is going on down here?" Keller's voice arrived in the galley seconds before he did.

Jo pushed herself up to her feet. "Pete is the biggest jerk I've ever met."

Keller chuckled even though the depth of his anger was etched in the lines of his face. "I don't think that's front page news."

"She dumped coffee in my lap," Pete said.

"He told me to bake him a cake!" She clamped her jaw and tried to lunge again. Keller put his arms up between them, pressing on Jo's shoulder. "I warned you what you signed up for."

He then flipped his attention to Pete. "And, I don't expect you to treat her any different that you would a new guy, but she's not here to be your momma."

As the two relaxed, Keller did too, stepping back and addressing the whole crew. "We're not even to the grounds yet! I don't have to tell you what our quota is and how important it is that both of my boats make their numbers quickly and efficiently. In order to do that, I need a crew who can bury their differences and work hard. Do I make myself clear?"

After a hushed round of yes sirs, Keller leveled his gaze on Pete. "Clean yourself up, for crying out loud." He then turned to Jo. "The coffee smells good. Is there any left?"

She nodded. "I'll bring a cup up for you."

* * * *

Back in the wheelhouse, Keller settled into the captain's chair. After he double-checked the coordinates on the GPS, he pushed on the throttle. The engine roared out its power and the boat propelled forward.

"Why do you keep it so dark in here?"

Jo's voice came from behind him. With each step she took, he could feel her getting closer, but resisted the urge to turn and take her in. "It's easier to see at night when I keep it dim inside." He took the cup from her. "Thanks."

She nodded an acknowledgement to his response, and pointed to the other seat. "You mind if I sit up here for a while?"

After what he'd just put an end to downstairs, she had good reason to ask, but giving her shelter would make her more of a target to the other men, and tempt his own desires. "I don't care, but avoiding the guys isn't going to get them to treat you any different."

She boosted herself up into the chair, and gazed out on the open water. "I'll worry about later when it comes. Now, I just want some quiet time. I don't think that Pete knows how to shut his mouth."

"Aw, he's an alright guy."

"He's a class A jerk!"

"He's a fisherman."

From the corner of his eye he could see her shrug, pull her feet up to the edge of the seat and wrap her arms around her knees. "So are you and Graham, and you don't act like Neanderthals all the time."

"He can be a little crass, maybe even vulgar; but he works hard, is aware of his surroundings, and keeps his head down. If I had two crews full of Petes, I'd have two well-run boats."

"You don't care how he treats other people?"

"It's not up to me how he was raised."

"But it's your boat. You don't think his attitude reflects on you?"

Keller couldn't stop the laugh, even though he knew she was serious. "This is a fishing boat, not a fortune-five-hundred company. I warned you what it was going to be like. Believe me, if you were a new guy on the boat, he'd be giving you just as much shit."

"It's not right."

"Maybe not, but this world is built on tradition. There's a code. If you want Pete's respect, you have to earn it."

She slid her fingers through her hair, and pulled a strand back from behind her ear, wrapping it around her finger. "I don't really care if he respects me or not."

"Permission to enter your wheelhouse, Captain?" Graham's voice came from behind them.

"Come on up."

Though he'd addressed Keller, Once inside the wheelhouse, Graham turned all his attention to Jo. "Enough, okay?"

"What are you talking about?" Jo said.

"You don't think Pete and Norm can figure out that you're up here complaining to Keller? Do you think that's going to make things any easier on this trip?"

"That's not what I'm doing." She didn't raise her voice, or even give Graham one of her death glares, but there was a firmness and authority to her tone that made Keller's libido stand up and take notice.

He absolutely adored that she was tough as nails, even when she was facing off with him.

"You begged and pleaded to get on this boat. The only way you're going to get those guys to accept you is through your work. This is one game that you have to play by *our* rules."

She leaned further back in the seat, and watched the water out the front window. Keller couldn't help but think she looked like someone who was born and raised on a boat. The first-mate seat fit her like the tight jeans she wore.

Jo said, "I don't care what Pete thinks of me."

"Pete's an ass. Everyone knows that. What you're doing right now is only going to make things worse."

"What do you think I'm doing?"

"Hiding out under Keller's protective wing."

"Hey." Keller spun the seat around so he could look at Graham. "We're just talking."

Jo stopped fiddling with her hair and sat up straighter in the seat. "I have every intention of standing on my feet and doing the job I begged for, but I will not take his crap. He gets in my face and he's going to get my best right back."

Graham laughed as if he knew exactly what "her best" entailed. "I wouldn't expect any different."

Jo hopped down off the chair and started for the steps. "I guess I'm headed downstairs."

Keller called after her. "Just hold on a minute."

After she turned back to him, he continued. "We should be to the grounds in about twenty hours. Jo, I want you on deck three hours before that to start prepping bait. Graham, I want you out there training her."

"Yes, sir," Graham answered.

Jo didn't speak, but gave him a curt nod.

"And your hair," he paused, and took a moment to admire how it reached down and swayed around her hips. "It can't be down like that out there. Up. Tight. Under a hat. For safety."

"Of course," she said.

He flipped his attention to Graham. "Get out of my wheelhouse, and send Pete up, would ya?"

"Sure thing."

Keller shifted in the chair and waited. Not even a full minute passed before he heard heavy steps ascending. "Come on in," he called out before Pete could go through the formality of asking permission.

"What's up, boss?"

"Take it down a notch or two with Jo."

"Why would I do that?"

"Because I said so. You don't have to treat her any different than you would another newbie, but knock off the sexist shit."

Pete took a step back, shaking his head. "So, lemmie guess. She was up here with the faucet on, and you can't stand to see a woman cry."

"You're wrong, and she didn't ask me to talk to you. She's not fragile, and I'm confident she can handle your crap—but I'm not going to have you treating her like a second class citizen because she's a woman."

"But it's okay if I pick on her for being green. Seems like you're splitting hairs to me."

Keller spun in the chair, giving Pete his full attention for the first time. "I put my ass on the line with you, Norm, Fred, and Graham. You're not losing anything out here, but if we don't fill the tanks in a timely manner, I could lose both boats. I need a crew that's tight. Do you hear me?"

"Sir," he said with a curt nod.

"Knock off the sexist shit. Am I clear?"

"Crystal, Sir."

Pete's last remark was soaked in sarcasm, but Keller dismissed him with a wave. An order was an order and above all else, Pete was a top-notch deck hand. He'd fall in line and do what he was told, even if it went against his nature.

CHAPTER TEN

A harsh reality pulled Jo from her pastel dreamland. Someone shook her shoulder. Opening her eyes, she saw Graham.

The boat was being pitched to and fro and the smell of dead fish, salt air, and testosterone assailed her senses. Her stomach tossed and turned like a washing machine.

"Come on, it's time to get to work. Get your gear on!"

She spun on the bunk, and put her feet on the floor, grateful that Graham had insisted on taking the bed above her in the small alcove that was separated from the other sleeping area. "Can I get sixty seconds of privacy to get dressed?"

"Sure. I'll pour you a coffee, and meet you at the door."

As Graham rounded the corner, Jo picked up her jeans off the floor and slipped them over her thermal underwear. Since the next twenty-four to thirty-six hours were going to see her filling bags and canisters with ground-up fish, she saw little need for fresh clothes. The large blue sweatshirt added a layer of comfort and heavy thermal socks went on before she laced up the lined, water-resistant boots.

She walked through the galley, bracing herself on the counter as the boat tossed again. Stumbling around another corner, Jo found Graham fully suited holding both travel mugs of coffee. "Come on. Step on it."

She slipped on her rain gear and then took one of the cups from Graham. A single sip was all she managed to take before he pushed open the door, and she got her first look at the Bering Sea in all its venomous glory.

A three hundred and sixty degree turn from the peaceful calm she'd got from watching the rolling waves from the wheelhouse just hours before.

"Not very welcoming is she, considering it's my first day."

Graham walked out onto the deck. "She's a cold, heartless bitch, and you haven't seen nothing yet."

As if to accent his words a huge swell crashed over the deck, spraying them. The water had to be just above the temperature that would make it ice, and a tremble racked her body. She used her gloved hand to push as much water off her face as possible. The smell of the ocean wasn't as overpowering as described by her father and Graham. Even though she worked in the offices, she'd endured worse odors in the cannery. They had a way of permeating walls. But the bitter cold was already biting through the gear, leaving goose bumps on her flesh.

"Sorry about that, you two." Keller's voice came over the speakers at each corner of the deck. "It's rough this morning. Be careful."

"Has he been up all night?" Jo asked.

Graham shook his head. "Fred drove for about four hours. Keller just got back in the chair. We need to bring up some boxes of herring and put them in the bin. We also need a few totes of the cod, so we can make up some strings."

"I'll grab the herring."

"Good, fill the rack. And Jo, take short, sure steps. You'll get your sea legs before too long, but until you do, be careful."

"Okay," was all she could say. As he'd suggested, all of her focus was needed to cross to the bait-fridge without losing her balance.

* * * *

Keller watched Jo move across the deck and the tension in his chest eased when he saw that she had the same agility she demonstrated on the dock. With her hair tucked neatly under her hat and the same bright yellow gear as the men, it might be hard to tell her apart from the rest of the crew, if not for her size.

Any other greenhorn would have had his name or a moniker written across the back of his coat in sharpie, just so Keller could keep a focused eye on the newbie, but it wouldn't be necessary with Jo. She was the shortest and slightest of the crew.

He'd be able to pick her out of anywhere.

Up and down the four steps to the bait area she went. Working efficiently and bringing up three boxes with each trip. He couldn't ask any more of any man on the crew, and had to admit she was probably in better physical shape than Fred or Norm.

Admiring her knack to handle herself on rough waters and her ability to do what the job required was allowed. He was her boss. She was an employee. At least that's what he told himself. It was the tightening low in his gut and the way his breathing sped up every time he laid eyes on her that caused guilt.

Another fallout from the night in the bar and that stupid bet.

78

He'd been silly drunk when she'd stumbled into his arms, and she was just as much impaired when she leaned against his shoulder. For a handful of seconds before she righted herself, that beautiful silk hair just under his chin ignited a spark inside him that was proving hard to extinguish.

Twenty-four hours later, his little stumble in the bar that landed him in her embrace had only fueled that flame.

From behind him the satellite phone rang. It shook his attention away from his growing lust, but clenched his heart with a new fear. It had to be Reese. Chances were better than even that bad news was about to be delivered before the first pot even hit the water.

He picked up the phone. "It's Keller."

"Hey, big brother."

"How's Carol," he asked while silently praying the doctors had successfully held the impending birth at bay.

"About the same. If the contractions don't start up again, they might send her home this afternoon. She'll be on complete bed rest for at least a couple of weeks."

Keller let out the deep breath that had caught in his throat. He knew things could change at any minute, but right now, he'd be thankful for each one that passed with no bad news. "We'll just keep hoping for the best."

"That's all we can do. Of course, Carol is out of her mind worried. The stress doesn't help. I can't tell you how glad I am that I stayed down here this year. I can't imagine if I'd been at sea when this happened."

"But you weren't. You were there, where you were supposed to be." Keller said the words to comfort his brother, but as he did he realized the truth to them. Never again would he be out-of-touch when someone he loved needed him. "Family comes first. I mean that. If something happens and you hesitate to call because of the fishing, I'm going to come home and kick your ass."

On the other end of the phone, Reese laughed. Keller saw through the attempt to break the tense mood. "Hopefully, we've turned a corner and it's all going to be all right."

With the serious subject discussed, the two chatted for a few more minutes as brothers, before Reese needed to leave because the doctor had arrived to examine Carol.

"I'll talk to you soon," Keller said, before hanging up the phone.

He spun his chair back to the controls. His gaze fell down to the deck. Though he'd still focused on the sea while talking to his brother, he hadn't kept an ever-watchful eye on Jo. A sudden wave of guilt crashed on him. It'd be so easy for her to get hurt, especially in these first few days while she was still getting used to the motion of the boat.

He needed to keep one eye on her at all times.

If anything happened, the blame would fall square on him. The responsibility was huge, and when he accepted the role of captain, he knew what that meant.

For all his men.

The side of him that was just a man worried even more about protecting this woman from the dangers of the sea.

Keller shook his head, refocusing his gaze. He couldn't be seeing it right. At least a dozen bait bags were filled and hanging and Jo appeared to be doing the task on her own. Graham kept an eye on her while he strung the cod. At the rate they were going they'd complete the job in half the time he'd allowed.

Don't get excited. This is the easy stuff.

Prepping bait was not, by any means, the difficult part of the job. And being sure-footed was either something a person came by or they didn't. It depended on their center of gravity and if they knew how to maximize it. The real test would come when she was baiting pots. Still, he gave her two checks in the plus column for her work this morning.

He picked up the radio's mike. "Great job, you two. Give me ten more of each and then come in and warm up."

Graham turned and gave Keller a thumbs up but he waited with anticipation as Jo spun on her heels, met his gaze, and nodded.

* * * *

"Graham, I'm pulling you off the deck to start dinner. Ten more pots gang and you'll have a three hour break." Keller's voice boomed over the speakers, cutting her flesh the same as the wind. Jo didn't need Keller or anyone else to tell her how many pots were left; she'd been counting them down since the beginning.

She leaned against the box, her hands gripping the wood rail as the boat tossed up and back. Her eyes locked on a focal point, she rode it out. The contents of her stomach stayed where they belonged this time.

Grabbing another bait bag and string of cod, she crossed the deck back to the launcher, staying on the mark Graham had showed her until the pot was secure and Pete and Norm had the doors open. She then pulled herself up into the iron cage, hooked on the bait as she'd been taught and slid back out. Moving as fast as possible and focusing on the iron bars in front of her face instead of the dark sky beyond it helped to keep the motion sickness in check.

Nine more prospect pots until she had a break.

"One good thing about her being so tiny is she does slide up into those pots easily."

Did Norm just paid me a compliment?

She fought the urge to smile in appreciation and stuck to her original plan—head down, mouth shut—and made her way back to the bait bin.

Pete chimed in. "I'd rather see her sliding in and out of my bed."

Ignore him.

She warned herself even though her fists clenched tight. The boat heaved again and she grabbed the bin to stay upright. Letting her gaze flow toward the rail, she got a look at the large crest before it crashed down, soaking both deckhands.

"Sorry about that one, guys." Keller's voice reverberated over the microphone, but sarcasm soaked his words as heavily as the men were now drenched from the sea.

Had Keller purposely showered Pete for his rude remarks?

"Come on, Jo. They're waiting on you." Keller barked from his warm, dry wheelhouse and Jo cursed again. Grabbing two more lines and crossing the deck for the forty-second time.

Lying flat on her back inside the metal pot, she tried to focus on her work: two hooks to the bar and slide out, but to her right, she saw that Pete stared down at her. A swarmy look glazed his eyes. When she darted her gaze away from him, she imagined a wave crashing over her, like the one that had just doused the guys. Her hands began to shake. Her chest tightened with panic.

Damn it Jo, you've come too far today to lose it now. You're almost done with this shift.

"Come on, baby, just work those hooks like they're the buttons on my jeans."

Pete's poke twisted into her like a rusty screw. With the bag and string secure, she gripped the bar, and pushed herself out of the cage.

With Graham inside, Pete was taking advantage of every moment that he could use to play with her head. Knowing that was what was happening didn't make it easier.

Nothing could make this an effortless job, but she'd known that going in.

Again the boat heaved, this time sweeping her feet out from under her. She landed ass-first on the cold, hard deck. As the bait box moved away from her, she reached out and gripped the leg of the table with all her might before the ice cold water came atop of her and sucked her toward the rail.

"Are you alright, Jo?" Keller's voice rang out through the speakers again.

Still gripping the leg of the bait table, the shivers that plagued her had grown to full out tremors. With her face soaking wet, no one would notice her tears, but still she fought to suppress them as she unwrapped one hand in order to give Keller a thumbs up, before pulling herself to her feet.

"Pete? Norm?"

Jo didn't look to the deck.

"Everything good, Fred?"

Fred was on a little higher and somewhat dryer ground behind the hydraulics, that wave had probably done little more than sprayed him.

Eight more pots.

Jo went back to the grind, grabbing the strings, and turning toward the pot.

Keller's voice cut the air again. "The weather's really turning, guys. Let's step it up and get these last pots in the water so I can get you off deck."

Step it up?

He couldn't mean go faster. Weren't they working at top speed now?

Inside the pot she went. Even though it was easily big enough to hold her and one of the large guys on deck, she felt claustrophobic. Her hands trembled. The clips clanked against the metal bar.

"Come on, Jo. Didn't you hear Keller? We got to step it up."

Norm again.

"What do you think I'm doing?" *Click. Click.* Both hooks in place, she pushed herself out, but instead of planting her feet on the ground, they slid out from under her and down she went. This time her skull crashed against the launcher.

Shit!

She gripped her now throbbing head and curled herself up.

"Damn it! Get up!" Pete yelled at her, nudging at her leg with his foot.

"You can't stay down!" Norm's voice followed. "Get up."

From the speaker came Keller's two-cents. "All right, Jo. Come inside, I'll send Graham out to finish up."

No!

Failing wasn't an option! Not with only seven pots left. She pushed herself to her feet, waving her arms. "I'll finish. I can do it." She tried to run, but with the toss of the boat and the water thickening toward ice, sliding was more like it.

"Jo. You're done. Get your ass inside." Keller's voice boomed again.

Turning back toward the launcher, she screamed. "I can finish this!" The pain cut through her head like red-hot knives and her vision blurred. Was that from the bump or the tears clouding her eyes? She blinked in rapid succession. Pete would not see her cry.

The pain!

She couldn't show these Neanderthals how vulnerable she felt.

Hurts so bad!

She'd never prove their sexist, old-fashion stereotypes to be true.

In and out, smooth and fast.

She pointed her mind at each step in the process, giving each movement her full concentration. As she slid out, Norm grabbed her arm, turned her toward him and wiped his fingers against her cheek.

She twisted and fought to pull away from him, until he showed her his fingers. They were coated with blood, *her* blood. Norm then raised his hand up toward Keller "She's bleeding."

"Damn it, Jo. Get inside, now!" The absolute order in his voice shook her core. She nodded once before heading for the hatch.

Just before she was close enough to reach for the door, it pushed open and Graham was coming out.

"Are you okay?" he asked.

She nodded. "Yes... No... Yes."

He patted her shoulder as she went by him. "Top notch job for a greenhorn. I mean that. Don't feel bad."

How could she not? The first day out and she'd failed. Only seven more pots and she would have gone the distance. Instead she'd been called off the mound at the bottom of the ninth so the old, reliable pitcher could finish the game.

Inside, she pulled off her boots, and then the rest of her rain gear, saving the hat for last. When she looked down and saw just how much blood soaked the once blue yarn, her stomach flipped and her knees buckled.

Leaning her weight against the wall on one hand, she pulled the bobby pins out of her hair, letting it fall and carefully felt her head, wincing in pain and keenly aware that the wetness was from blood and not the sea water. The closer she got to the point where her head had hit the launcher, the more intense the pain got. At the destination she felt a large, open gash in the flesh.

"Jo! Get up here!" Keller called out. Gone was the anger and conviction that he'd used to get her off the deck. With this bark, she could hear fear and genuine concern.

She inhaled deeply and let it out slowly to find her center, and then moved through the galley and up the steps to the wheelhouse. "How bad is it?" Keller asked as she crossed the threshold.

"I'm fine. I wish you wouldn't have pulled me in."

His eyes were focused on the deck, only breaking for a brief dart to the radar. After he hit the button that sounded the buzzer telling the crew to dump the pot, he turned around and looked at her. "Good, God, Jo. You're white as a ghost. Come here."

She had to laugh, even though she knew he'd reached for the cliché, white wasn't a usual description for her dark skin. "Somehow I don't think it's that bad." She followed his order, moving closer.

Again he was fixated on the job on the deck. Keeping one eye of protection on his crew and one on the radar. Such precision as he waited until the boat hit the exact spot he wanted and then his waiting finger depressed the button, signaling Fred to launch the pot and giving him a moment's break to turn back to her. "Are you nauseous?"

"Not any more than I was before I hit my head."

"Seasick?"

She nodded. Now her eyes were fixated on the guys below. They were working like a machine. Graham moved in and out at twice the speed she had, and he didn't hesitate with the clips. *Clank, clank,* and they were in place.

"Can I see the wound?"

His request shook her out of the descending state of failure that was encasing her and she pulled her hair apart and leaned over, biting her tongue to keep herself from crying out at the pain.

He touched her hair, below her hand, and moved his fingers over it like a comforting caress. She wanted to lean into his touch before she corrected herself. *He's looking at your foolish injury, not seducing you, bonehead.*

"It's bleeding like a stuck pig, but any head wound will do that. It's not that deep. Hurts?"

"Like a bitch."

"You're trembling?"

She looked down at herself. So she was. She'd been doing it for so long, it wasn't registering in her brain anymore. "I've never been so cold."

"Why don't you take a hot shower? Wash the blood out of your hair and change into dry clothes. We'll let these pots soak for a few hours before we start to pull 'em up."

"Graham said the showers were few and far between."

"We try to conserve resources, but that wound needs to be cleaned. And you can't walk around with blood in your hair."

He pushed the button, and she saw it was the last pot going into the water. They'd pushed through those last few in what seemed like record time. Disgrace weighted on her shoulders. "I'll just wash my hair out in the sink."

He pulled the throttle half-way back, and the props slowed. Into the mic he said, "That's it guys. Clean up the deck, then come in and eat."

He turned to Jo. "There's no way you can wash your hair in the tiny sink. Seriously, it's okay. Take a shower." After she nodded, he continued. "When you go down there, hold your chin up, okay. You did a great job for a greenhorn. I couldn't have asked for better."

"I was slow."

"There's a learning curve."

"I-I-I didn't finish." She cringed at the whine in her voice. She'd tried so hard to conceal it.

"I never expected you to. Honestly, I thought I'd have to give you a break after twenty pots. The average newbie would never have hung in there for forty-three. I'm amazed with your performance. Now, I'm ordering you to take a shower, get some dinner. Feel good about the work you put in."

She'd learned one thing thus far. Keller didn't say things he didn't mean. His compliments eased the sting of defeat.

CHAPTER ELEVEN

Keller heard the crew bustling in the galley and called down, ordering Jo up the steps before settling down in the captain's chair and examining the charts and radar.

"You wanted to see me?"

He glanced up over his shoulder, than back to the charts, forcing himself not to stare at her, not wanting to show any of the desire churning his gut. "How are you feeling? Better?"

"I *am*."

"How's your head? Are you nauseous?"

"It hurts and my stomach's doing backflips, but I don't think it's because I bumped my head."

He gave a motion with his hand, telling her to come closer, but kept his gaze on the paperwork in front of him. Anything to get closer to her.

Did that make him as chauvinistic as Pete?

When she stood in front of him, the crisp, clean scent of the cheap deodorant soap he'd bought for the boat assailed him. On anyone else, he found it overpowering and more than a little obnoxious. On her, it made him weak in the knees. He swallowed the lump in his throat. "Can I have a look?"

How he hoped she didn't notice that his pitch was raised. He spun the chair, and she stepped even closer bending at the waist.

"I'm sorry, I haven't pinned up my hair yet."

"That's okay." He choked the words out. In fact, it was all the better. Her long, silky tresses caressed the palm of his hands as he carefully separated the strands. A goose-egg sat angrily on her scalp, but the cut had scabbed over. "You sure you're not dizzy?"

She stood and tossed her hair over her shoulders. "I'm positive. Really. If the guys can go back out to work, well, then I want to too."

"I'm not going to stop you."

She smiled wide. "Then I'll get my gear on."

"Hold on just a minute. Graham or Fred will give you full directions when you get on deck, but I want to give you a quick rundown. When the pot comes up, they'll dump the contents on to the table. When the launcher returns to its down position, crawl in, pull out the old bait lines. If we're resetting, hook on two new strings. If we need to move it, we'll stack it without bait. Okay?" He was rambling. But he couldn't shut up. Didn't want her to walk away.

"Sure. How will I know if we're resetting or moving?"

"I'll let you guys know over the loudspeakers. Pay attention."

* * * *

At the bottom of the steps, Jo found the galley empty and could hear the guys putting on the gear in the small nook by the door. "I'll be right there."

"There's a coffee for you on the table. Drink it fast," Graham said.

She dug into her pocket, coming back with six bobby pins. Dropping them to the table she pulled her hair back as if she was going to put it in a ponytail, but instead twisted a few times and began wrapping it around like a bun. After she made one complete circle, she picked up a pin and pushed it into her hair, cursing as it broke. Looking at the piece still in her hand, she could see it had rusted clean through. Further inspection of the pins on the table showed they all had rusted. From one day exposed to the sea water.

Now what am I going to do?

Remembering an elastic pony tail holder in her duffle bag, she made quick steps to her bunk and dug around in the bag until she came back with the band. Securing the pony tail, she repeated her motions from before—without the pins—and when her hair was in a neat pile, pulled her hat down over it.

Back in the galley she picked up the travel mug from the table and took a long sip from it, thankful that it had cooled off enough she could gulp the contents. Two more drinks between putting on her gear and the cup was empty and she was out on the deck.

"Hey, start prepping some bait. With any luck we'll be on the crab and resetting these," Graham said.

A scan of the deck told her the others had already begun working. Boxes of herring were stacked by her table, so she got straight to work.

The roll of the waves seemed tamer than she was last on deck, and she easily kept her balance. Her stomach sloshed less too, allowing her to perform the mindless task of bait prep without having to give too much concentration to her surroundings. Her mind wandered back up to the wheelhouse, and the way he'd touched her hair.

It was probably nothing. After-all he was checking out the knot on her head, but he'd used light hands and a tender caress and her instinct had been to melt into him.

Let him wrap his strong arms around her, and just absorb her problems.

Now aren't I turning into Cinderella?

Never before had she needed a charming prince, so why, exactly, was she looking at Keller that way, especially since he was cut from the same cloth as her father? As the rest of these guys.

No roots. Drawn to the sea, the only mistress any of them would truly love. No home life. No family.

To be involved with Keller would mean spending her life alone, as she had her childhood.

The thought of inviting him over for dinner in her father's presence brought forth a laugh. Sure, Lark thought Keller was a good guy—but there's no way he'd stand silent and let the Nordic prince carry away his little girl. She had to wonder if anyone would measure up to Graham in her father's eyes.

"Come on, Jo, One's coming up?" Norm shouted from the rail.

Crap!

How had she blocked out her surroundings for so long? She grabbed two strings and covered the distance between her station and the launcher.

Thick tension hung in the air as the bailer slowly grinded, pulling the pot closer to the surface.

"Damn it! I knew it!" Pete cursed. "It's light. I guarantee you that thing is empty."

"How can he know that?" Jo asked Norm who stood just to her right.

"You can hear it. When it's pulling a heavy pot, it sounds different."

If Pete was right, every one of these guys would blame her for the bad fishing. It wouldn't matter that she'd pulled her weight when they were setting them.

The pot broke the water and when it was lifted so she could see, her heart dropped. Not any more crab than she could count on two hands. She slid a few steps back and let them empty them on the table.

"Three keepers," Graham mumbled under his breath even before the pot was secure.

"Stack it," Keller's voice rang through the speakers unnecessarily. Everyone knew what the order would be. She didn't have to see his face to know he was just as disappointed as the rest of the crew.

Jo dropped the bait in her hand and vaulted herself into the pot, pulling down the strings of hardly-touched bait.

Norm met her as she approached the table. "Grab a tote and drop the used strings in it. When you get a chance clean up the string and cans and dump the old bait."

After the last shift, the drill was pounded into her head. Three minutes. In that time she needed to complete the task list Norm dictated, and be ready to climb into the next pot.

Graham picked up the fresh bait. "Here, we'll clip this set to the edge of the table in case we get lucky on the next one."

Eye contact was enough to acknowledge him.

She returned to the mark, just as the next pot cleared the rail. Her left leg began to bounce. This one had less than the previous.

"Damn! Stack it!" Keller's voice cut through the air.

"Tell me this isn't unusual," Jo said to Graham,

knowing he was the only one she could trust for complete honesty. He wouldn't fall prey to the superstitions as easily as the others would.

"It happens, but with Keller in the big chair, not very often."

As she grabbed the edge of the pot and vaulted herself up inside the iron cage, the cold permeated the thermal gloves. Jo kept her eyes focused on the clips as she pulled them free and slid out.

"Don't fall again, sugar."

Same old Pete, but she didn't expect different. Fear and frustration dissolved her better judgment and the ability to censor herself. "Shut the hell up, asshole."

Pete grabbed her arm and spun her back to him, "What did you say to me?"

Jo pushed up on her toes and stretched her back as taut as possible, but still failed in her attempt to meet his eyes. "I said, Shut. The. Hell. Up. Are you as deaf as you are stupid?"

Giving her a shove, Pete turned his attention up toward Keller. "If you want any chance at filling this boat, you better sacrifice your little nymph to the crab gods."

Jo felt her breaking point snap like a dry twig and tossed the bait strings on the deck. She lunged at him again, gripping the vinyl of his jacket between her fingers. "Do you think you're man enough to do it?"

Pete locked his arms around her forearms, trying to hold her back from him. "Graham, get your girlfriend off me before I throw her overboard."

The fact that the engines were in idle didn't even register for Jo, until she felt arms come around her waist, pulling her away from Pete, just as Graham stepped between them, pushing Pete back.

"What in the hell is wrong with you, Pete? Beating up on women now?" Graham screamed.

"She attacked me!"

"Because you've been pushing her since the moment she stepped on the boat," Graham said, but as she rolled her head to the side and felt the wool of Keller's sweater against her cheek, the rest of the boat began to fade away.

A clean, linen scent enveloped her, probably from the fabric softener the sweater had been treated to before being packed for the trip. The muscles in his arms were tense and she felt protected and warm there. But, she didn't need a protector. Pete would never respect her until she stood tall without Keller or Graham stepping in.

"Let me go, Keller. I'm going to rip him apart."

"You'll do no such thing!" he screamed, his voice as icy as the wind burning her cheeks. He set her feet back on the ground and loosened his grip. "Both of you. The wheelhouse. Now!"

As she started for the door, she heard Keller tell Fred to start breakfast. "We might just as well use this time efficiently."

* * * *

Keller gripped the door handle, but stopped just short of opening it. Nothing gnawed at his stomach more than a bad vibe hanging over his boat, and the tension between Jo and Pete was about as bad as it got. He knew what had to be done, doing it was going to be the hard part.

Steeling himself, he pulled the door open and marched through the galley and up the steps. There he found Jo and Pete in opposite chairs staring daggers at each other.

"What in the hell was that about?"

Pete clenched his jaw. "She jumped me!"

"He's lying," Jo said.

"Jo," Keller interjected, withdrawing some of his anger. "I saw you lunge at him."

"He won't shut his damn mouth. It never stops with the snide remarks and the sexist garbage."'

Keller pivoted. "I warned you about that the other night."

"All I said was 'don't fall.' I was expressing concern."

"You lying sack-of—" Jo stopped and inhaled sharply. "It was *how* he said it, with the 'sugar' on the end. And yesterday, after you called Graham in—"

"What are we—in the third grade?" Pete said. "Tattle to the teacher, little pet!"

Teacher of a couple of snot-nosed Kindergarteners is exactly how Keller felt. It was passed time to put these two in opposite corners for a time out. He slammed his hand against the wall before jamming his finger in Pete's face. "Stop! Now! No More! I can't have this tension. There's too much riding on this season and eating a hole in my stomach. Crap like this is only making it worse. We *have* to move as one team!"

"And you!" He spun to Jo, locked in on her big brown eyes and felt his resolve quiver just like his knees. His mouth went dry, but he pushed the words out. "You can't start physical fights on this boat. Especially on the deck. I can't believe this is even an issue. Why would you lunge at him like that?"

"I warned you I wouldn't just sit by and let him attack me."

The fierce pride raging on her face melted his anger. Why was this happening? He didn't want to be lusting after her. Didn't need the complication. He wanted to be angry, damn it! "I'm not saying lay down and take it, but you can't be pushing and shoving and hitting. It's too dangerous. Too easy for one of you to get tossed right overboard. I won't have it on my boat. Do you hear me?"

"Yes, sir." She jutted her left hip toward him and pointed her chin over her right shoulder.

"Thank you. Fred's fixing breakfast, since we had to stop anyway. You guys eat quickly and get back on deck. We're getting a few so I don't think we're too far off the crab. Let's see if we can find 'em."

They both nodded and were almost out of the room, when Keller couldn't help himself and called her back. "Don't listen to any of those boneheads if they start blaming you."

Her shoulders squared and she planted her hands on her hips. "Why would it be my fault?"

"We're you listening to me? I just said it's not." He gripped the back of his seat, and then spun it around and climbed in. He reached for the package of cigarettes, but then tossed them back down. "You know that fishermen are a superstitious breed. Some of the guys might start saying that you're a bad luck charm. Don't listen to them."

Even though he was doing his best not to look at her, he could see her from the corner of his eye. At his words, her posture loosened and those bricks began to crumble. She took a step closer to him. "I thought you were one of those guys who believed in that stuff."

He flicked his fingers against the cellophane package, reminding himself they were weeks old and probably tasted like garbage. He didn't need to start smoking again. He'd battled too hard to quit. "I'm the captain. I decided where to set those pots. This is all on me. No one else is to blame."

"How much trouble are you in if you don't find them?"

"I'm going to put us on the crab, I don't have another choice."

"I have no doubt." She spun and started for the steps, but as her hand grazed the opening, she paused. "I'm very proud of you, by the way."

"For what?"

"Not smoking. I know it's hard. My dad's been trying to quit since last year. Unsuccessfully. He thinks that I believe he's not smoking, but I can smell the smoke on his clothes."

He tapped his foot against the floor. "I never should have started. I only did it to try and get the others to stop calling me a kid my first year on the boat."

"But you've stopped now. I'd hate to think of you with all the same health problems my father has."

There it was, another parallel between their lives. "My dad too. The cigarettes were a big part of what got him in the end."

Jo rotated against the door, putting herself back in the room. "I keep forgetting it hasn't been that long."

Keller could feel his throat closing and coughed, hoping it would clear the pain away. "Eighteen months."

"It's got to be tough to be on this boat without him."

"Sometimes. It was a lot worse last year. The crew still thought of me as a deckhand. I had to fight for the respect."

She bowed her head and some of her hair fell lose from its binds. "It's not just me. Is it? Everyone has to prove themselves."

"I'm sure they're being even harder on you because you're a woman, but it's just the way of the sea. No one gets respect handed to them."

"I'll try to keep my temper under wraps."

"Thanks. Go get something to eat so we can get back to work. Have one of the guys fill the thermos and bring me up a plate before you head back out."

CHAPTER TWELVE

Jo tried to gain traction, but the wet deck was icing up. Instead of fighting the momentum, she loosened her muscles and slid until she hit the bait table. Gripping the edge, she bent over at the waist. The scent of herring and cod guts did nothing to settle the tossing and turning of her stomach. Every muscle in her body screamed in pain, which shocked her because her flesh was numb from the cold.

"Jo! You okay?" Keller's voice rang out over the loudspeaker.

She gripped the edge of the table tighter, and lifted her right arm, giving a "thumbs up" toward the wheelhouse, but didn't turn. She didn't want him to see the misery on her face. If he did, he might call her in and she was determined to keep up with the men today. She swallowed the stomach acid bubbling to her throat before she began filling two bait pails.

The first string had been dismal. Pulling the pots and resetting them in a scatter-pattern had been tedious. The second string had proven better. However, the numbers were still modest according to Graham.

Fred had pointed out that modest was better than nothing.

They had stacked and moved that string a few miles north. This one was even better than the second. She'd been relieved to hear they were resetting, until she found out how much work that involved.

Hearing the grind of the block, she grabbed the bait setups and two cod strings and started back across the deck. She'd lost count of the pots, and had no idea how many more they had to pull and reset.

Graham slipped in next to her, coiling the line. She leaned in and spoke loud enough to be heard, but hopefully quiet enough that no one else would feel the need to give their two cents. "How much longer?"

He flipped his attention to her, but then quickly back to his task-at-hand. "We work until Keller says we're done."

"But this is the last string? Right?"

"That's up to Keller. We might break, we might head back to the beginning and start pulling again." As the pot cleared the rail, a large smile lit up his face. "Look at that! That ought to cheer the ol' man up."

Fred and Pete pushed the doors open and large, red crab dumped into the table. Her eyes scanned and she tried to guess—forty of them maybe? She then followed the pot as it was locked into place. Once she was given an all clear signal, she slid into the pot and switched out the bait setups while others began sorting crab. She tried to push away Graham's insistence that Keller may keep them working after this string.

She'd no sooner slipped from the pot and released the iron bar, when the lift went up dumping it into the sea. The movement and the sound alerted her defenses and she dropped to one knee, ducking her head under her arm.

"Step it up, Jo! You need to keep up with the pace, not set it." Keller's voice chastised from up top.

Her lower lip curled between her teeth and she stood. Bringing the second set of bait to the table saved her steps and allowed her to help the others finish sorting the bounty from the previous pot.

Graham squeezed her shoulder. "You're doing good."

"Pete's trying to kill me."

He leaned over the table, and looked back over his shoulder so he could meet her gaze. His lips flattened in a narrow line. "You're being ridiculous."

"I'd barely cleared the pot and he was dumping it."

"That's how it works around here. Drop the martyr complex and do your work."

Her shoulders tightened and a wave crashed over the side of the boat, spraying her and the others with icy salt water. The chill climbed her spine and the urge to purge the contents of her stomach washed over her again. She gripped the edge of the table and pushed back, lowering her body, stretching her back as a preventative measure. If she was going to puke better it hit the deck than the table.

"Jo! You okay?" Keller's voice shattered the air again. She unhooked the second bait setups and straightened her body, nodding toward the wheelhouse.

There was a long pause and then his voice cut the air again. "Five more pots and then you guys can grab some food while we turn and burn. After this pot I want Jo to come in and get the food around. Graham, rotate to her spot."

"Screw that," she whispered under her voice, thinking only Graham could hear her. "I'm finishing today."

"Just do what you're told!" Fred said. "This isn't a democracy. Keller's the dictator. Just. Do. What. You're. Told."

As Jo slipped into the empty pot and changed out the settings, acid burned a hole in her stomach. For the second time in two days, Keller was pulling her off the deck. And she'd thought they'd found some common ground this morning. Her fellow deck mates would never learn to respect her if he kept her from finishing a single shift.

She slid out of the pot and handed the empty strings to Graham, before turning for the cabin door.

"Damn it, Jo! Think before you use that mouth of yours!" he said.

One truth, Graham knew her. For a brief second, she considered following his advice and just doing what she was directed, but as she put her hand on the refrigerator door, her blood turned hot. There was no way she was going to let Keller pull her off the deck and put her in a housekeeping role. He was supposed to be different than Pete.

She took the steps two at a time, but as she hit the top. Keller's sharp words stopped her cold.

"Step one foot in my wheelhouse, and I'll fire you."

She bristled, his voice as cold as the sea spray. "But—"

He cut her off, but his eyes were focused on the sea in front of him and the deck below. "No! I know what you're thinking. I could see it your body language. And don't forget I can hear everything that's said down there." He pointed to the speakers above his head.

"I wanted to prove to everyone I could do the job today. And I can."

"I didn't call you away from the work. You guys are going to have about forty minutes while I head back to the first string. We use the breaks, eat when we can.

Every other crew member has taken on food prep. If I'd asked anyone other than you, it would be showing favoritism. Now, are you a member of this crew or not?"

He was right. In her attempts to fight for a position, she succeeded in forgetting Keller's number one rule. Everyone does their job—the one the captain assigns.

"I'm sorry."

"I don't want to hear 'I'm sorry.' The only thing I want to hear out of your mouth the rest of the day is 'yes, sir.' Is that clear?"

"Yes, Sir." The words tasted like bile, she was never really the subordinate type. They were also weighted in guilt for her shortsightedness.

"Thank you. The rest of the crew will be in to eat in about five minutes. Can you get the sandwich fixings out?"

"Yes, sir." She tapped her fingers against her pants and pushed down her frayed nerves.

"Have someone bring me up a plate before you head back out."

"Yes, sir," she repeated again and turned; taking the steps at the same speed she'd climbed them. Disappointing him hurt as much as her aching muscles.

Jo set the food on the table. When she heard the back door fly open and the men's voices and laughter filter in, she made herself a sandwich and took it out to the small alcove, sitting on the bench.

She took a bite of the turkey and cheese sandwich, but had to force herself to swallow it. Her stomach sloshed to and fro with the movement of the boat and even though the cabin was a comfortable temperature, goose bumps still coated her arms. As she attempted a second bite, she noticed her hands still trembled, but not from the cold. Her nerves were bare wires and with every obstacle she hit, they touched, short circuiting her system.

"Are you okay?"

She looked up over her shoulder to see Graham in the doorway. "I will be. I just needed a few minutes all my own."

"You want me to leave you alone?"

She slid a little further down the bench and shook her head.

He sat close, and took a bite of his food and chewed it thoroughly before speaking. "You're doing good."

"Doesn't feel like it."

"I know. It was a long time ago, but I remember what it's like being the new kid. Trust me."

"I don't think I've ever been so tired in all my life."

He slipped his arm through hers, and she leaned on him, laying her head on his shoulder. "If you weren't exhausted, I'd be worried. Everyone is. You're handling it. Be proud of that...but you need to let go of some things."

"I'm a deckhand and he's the captain."

"Exactly. He lectured you?"

She nodded and pulled herself upright. Graham moved his arm, draped it over her shoulder in comfort, making her thankful to have her best friend by her side. "I can't imagine doing this without you here."

"You don't have to worry about that, but I have no doubt that you'd be fine. A lot of new guys have come on this boat and haven't held up as well as you."

"I'm worried about Dad." The words slipped from her mouth, but saying them relieved that storm brewing in her stomach. She'd tried to write off the knots as seasickness, but now knew it was homesickness.

"Your mom's friend is there. She's taking care of him."

"I trust my mom's judgment, but I know my father. He isn't making this easy on that woman."

"When does you dad make anything easy?"

"He's so mad at me for coming out here. I'm afraid he's taking it out on me, by not following doctor's orders. Like he did when I went to visit my mom."

"Lark's pride is hurt, but he wouldn't hurt himself to prove a point. He'll get over it. When neither of you have to worry about the mortgage anymore, he'll get better."

"I hope you're right."

"I am. Just wait and see."

The sound of Keller clearing his throat filtered in from the doorway. Jo looked up and shuddered under his angry gaze.

"Gear up. I want to check on this first string. If we're not catching, I want to move them."

"Sure thing." Graham answered.

"Yes, sir." Jo spit out the ordered response and then stood and reached for her jacket.

As Keller walked away from Graham his stare stayed locked on the captain. "Go on out with the others. I'll be right there."

Jo grabbed his sleeve. "Don't get in trouble defending me."

He flashed her a smile. "Wasn't planning on it."

* * * *

"Can I talk to you for a minute?"

Keller didn't have to swivel his chair or look over his shoulder, he knew the sound of Graham's voice, could feel him standing in the doorway of his wheelhouse. "I'll give you thirty seconds. Then, I want you on deck."

Keller kept his eyes focused on the clipboard and the sonar, Graham approached.

"Jo would never say anything to anyone but me, but she's worried about Lark. I just thought maybe after the shift, you could suggest she call home. It would make her feel better to talk to him."

Keller knew what it meant to worry about a parent. It was enough to get him to drop the clipboard and spin to Graham. "Any of you can call home anytime you want. You know that, right?"

"I do. Jo is too worried about proving she's tough enough to ask. She's been through a lot lately. I'm just afraid she's ready to crack."

Keller gave him a nod. He'd seen glimpses of Jo's tender side in the last few days. "Thanks for telling me."

As Graham left the room, Keller leaned back in his chair, and cursed himself for not recognizing Jo's agony for what it was. He'd seen how much Lark's health had gone downhill when he came to the docks. Jo had confided in Keller about it. Of course it was weighing heavy on her.

He knew what it felt like to have the Bering Sea between you and a sick parent and would make sure he encouraged Jo to call home, without letting her know it was Graham's idea.

Grabbing the candy bar sitting on the table next to him, he broke off a square of the dark chocolate. One eye on the rolling waves and one on the sonar, he tried to push the guilt out of his mind.

Why did I yell at her like that?

He knew the answer to that question, but didn't want to admit it, not even to himself. He'd gone down to apologize for being harsh, but when he'd seen Jo leaning up against Graham, an emotion he didn't like—jealousy—had bubbled up like indigestion after a bowl of Fred's three-alarm chili. The only arm he wanted draped over her shoulder was his own.

Seeing Graham in the place he coveted sent his mind spinning. Counting the number of times he'd heard Lark call Graham son, or refer to him as his soon-to-be son-in-law would be like counting the grains of sand on a beach.

Absolutely pointless.

Keller knew it was just as futile to lay hopes that he'd ever be the one to hold Jo close.

Good fishermen were married to the sea, and women like Jo wanted and deserved a whole lot more than a man whose obligations kept him away. That ruled both he and Graham out as a good partner for Jo.

CHAPTER THIRTEEN

"Don't you ever sleep?"

A sweater, hanging almost to her knees, covered her most intimate areas. Thermal underwear shielded her legs.

"I'll be going to sleep soon. I want to get a little closer to the next string and then I'll have Pete keep watch."

"Then I guess you don't want any coffee."

"No." He waited for her to speak again. Say something. When she didn't he continued. "You should be sleeping while you can. When I get up, we're going to be grinding for a long while."

"I have been. I just got up for some water and thought I'd see if you needed anything."

He glanced over his shoulder again and saw her standing so still just outside the door, the small plastic bottle clutched in her left hand. "You can come in and sit down...if you want."

She crossed the room and climbed up into the chair opposite of him. Despite her short stature, he couldn't help but steal a glance of her legs wrapped in the grey cotton fabric. Thermal underwear shouldn't make his heart race the way it did when she wore it.

"I don't want to cross any lines with you, Sir—"
Ugh! So stubborn.

She wasn't going to let go of his rant from this morning. "Okay, You can stop with the sir."

"But you said—"

Another sideways glance and he was snagged by her large brown eyes. They clearly gave away the sarcasm that only tainted her words. "I know what I said. I was angry and trying to make a point."

She leaned back in the chair and pulled her foot up to the edge wrapping her arms around her knee. "I'm sorry. You took a big risk by letting me come out here, and I haven't been acting very grateful. Believe me, I am."

He swiped his hand down his jaw line. "We had a deal and I'll keep my end of it."

"I appreciate that."

He nodded his head and kept his eyes on anything but her. Taking in her body would push him over the edge. Reaching over he broke off a piece of the candy bar and popped it in his mouth, then picked up the wrapper and handed it in her direction. "Would you like a piece?"

"Thanks."

After breaking off a square and tasting it she moaned, the way he imagined she would if he were kissing her.

"That is *amazing*. I've never seen this brand before."

"It's Theo. The company is local to Washington."

"There are plenty of wrappers in the garbage here." Her voice held a light lilt.

She was teasing him and it tightened his gut the same as if she were dragging her fingers down his chest bone.

"I had to replace cigarettes with something." He patted his belly. "Unfortunately this habit has its downfalls too."

She hopped down from the seat and stepped closer to him, dropping the candy bar back to the table next to him. The smell of her, sweet and soft like delicate flowers drenched in clean salt water, tickled his nose.

"It's all right. A couple pounds would look good on you."

He felt his cheeks warm and bit the inside of his lip trying to suppress it. Blushing was more befitting one of his sisters and would totally squelch the image of tough captain he was going for. "You're teasing me."

Geez! That sounded weak!

"Maybe a little bit." She laughed and her hand brushed his shoulder as she took a couple of steps back and hopped up into the chair, leaning back against the leather. "I never used to understand why my dad and Graham seemed to love this so much."

Her eyes were fixated on the rolling waves, and for just a moment he noted how nice it would be to have a companion on these trips. "But you do now?"

"Sort of. Not the deckhand stuff. I hate that! But this. The peace of the night, the hum of the motor mixed with the motion of the sea. It's relaxing."

Keller would never describe twenty-foot waves as the "motion of the sea." Graham's words from earlier thumbed through his mind. He'd said she was stressed out from all of her responsibilities. *"Ready to crack,"* had been the words he'd used. If she found the hefty toss of these waves relaxing, life at home must have felt like a level five hurricane.

"Not everyone's cut out for this." He paused and waited for some type of response from her, letting his gaze flicker in her direction again. Her chin was resting on her upturned knees. Her stare fixated toward the window. "You've hung in there a lot better than I thought you would."

"Thanks," her voice was soft and distant, like she was drifting to sleep. Who could blame her? He was desperate for his own pillow and he'd been sitting in the chair instead of working on deck. Graham's request sounded in his head again. "We've been out here a few days now. Do you want to call home and check on Lark?"

Her eyebrows arched. He could see she was weighing her choices. It wasn't that complicated.

"The satellite phone is expensive."

"Don't worry about the cost. It's your father and his health. I *know* what you're going through."

"Are you sure it's okay?"

"I'm positive."

Jo's gaze drifted to the clock on the back wall. She must have decided it wasn't too late because she popped down off the chair again and went to the phone behind him, picking it up and dialing the number. She rested the phone on her shoulder, leaning her cheek into it. With her hands free, she pulled her long braid over the opposite shoulder and began to release the tie and unweave her hair.

Keller couldn't keep himself from stealing glances over his shoulder at her. When a relieved smile crossed her lips, he couldn't stop his own.

"Hi, Dad, how are you doing?"

Even though the phone wasn't connected to the wall, she paced back and forth in a short pattern not much wider than the back of his chair. He did his best not to eavesdrop on the conversation, difficult when she was standing just behind him.

Though the first few moments of Jo's conversation had been tense, she'd quickly softened in posture and voice and they'd moved on to easier topics than the fishing or his health.

"… I've got to get off the phone, Dad. Please, listen to the nurse and take care of yourself."

After she hung up the phone, Jo rounded his chair so she could look Keller in the eye. "Thank you for letting me call home. I feel so much better after talking to him."

"Glad to hear it. He's okay?"

"He says so. He sounded tired, but good." She paused, and looked out the front of the boat again. "I'm going to get a little more sleep. You should too. You look exhausted."

"Not any more than normal, but I am going to take a break soon."

It wasn't until after Jo had left the wheelhouse that Keller realized how thick and hot the air had been while she was there. Or should he say, how she made him feel?

He'd long given up the notion that lust had taken root because of alcohol. The more time he spent with her, the more he'd seen her soul, the more she stood her ground with him and the rest of the crew, the deeper that affection grew.

In just a handful of days he'd gone from not being able to imagine a woman working on his boat to not wanting to think about how lonely it was going to be next trip without her there.

* * * *

The numbers on the page began to blur together; Keller leaned back in the seat and rubbed his eyes. He glanced up at the clock and tried to do the math. How many hours had they been at it? He'd lost track at twenty-seven. It had to be in the neighborhood of thirty by now.

He glanced down to the deck, his crew like zombies. Two more pots and he was going to have to dash. The seas were picking up and the radio was announcing near hurricane-force winds and torrential seas. Nothing he'd ever fish in, even if Jo wasn't on the deck.

He eased back on the throttle. Pete's arm had to be numb from tossing the hook and Keller didn't want even a chance that Pete miss this one.

When the pot was safely on board, Keller picked up the microphone. "One more pot and then I want you to secure the deck and come in. We're going to duck and cover."

Or maybe we should just head for Dutch.

He tried again to add the column of numbers. He knew they were close to filling the tanks, but it would be better if they could go through the gear one more time.

On the other hand, I might be able to stay ahead of the storm running in.

Jo shouldn't be out here in the weather they had coming. Though she maintained a strong front, Keller could tell she was losing her battle with motion sickness and her nerves were stretched thin. She needed the forty-eight hour break an off load would give them.

If it were any other crew, I wouldn't even be thinking about going in.

Minimize costs. Maximize profits.

His father's words of wisdom echoed in his ears.

That made his decision. They'd lay anchor behind the small island while these pots soaked. They'd get some sleep, and some food. Then, make one last run through the gear. When the tanks were stuffed, they'd head to port.

Only after Jo had followed the rest of the crew into the cabin, could Keller let out the breath he'd been holding. His shoulders eased and his eyelids grew heavy.

Who knew that pure fear could fuel enough adrenaline to keep him awake?

He shifted his weight and pushed down on the throttle as he began to steer the boat around to the North.

Graham's voice called his name from the doorway behind him.

"Come," he paused for a moment, focusing on getting the boat on the right coordinates. "What's going on?"

"How bad is the weather going to get?"

"If I thought we could push through the gear one more time we would, but it's going to be too dangerous. We'll drop anchor until the storm passes."

"We're close to full. Maybe an off load makes more sense."

Keller leveled his gaze on Graham. It wasn't his style to question his captain, and Keller wasn't in the mood for the slightest amount of doubt. "I've made my decision."

"Did you take Jo into account? If you go in, you've fulfilled your bargain with her. The one trip would be over."

"I weighed all the options." He turned his chair so it was facing front. What he couldn't say aloud was that as much as he worried about her on deck, he wasn't ready to excuse her from the boat. "Even if I could move up our scheduled off-load time, it doesn't make any sense to go in before we're topped off."

"Just thought I'd mention it."

He knew Graham's concern didn't necessarily mean anything more than friendship, but it still needled the little green monster that had showed up inside Keller. The idea that he was fighting for Jo's attention or affection was absurd, especially since he'd kept his feelings to himself. "One more time through the gear, then we'll get her back on land."

He nodded and started down the steps. Keller then heard the sound of feet coming back up.

Graham again. "You've been in the chair for a long time. Do you want me to drive the boat?"

"Thanks, but you need the rest more than I do right now."

"You sure?"

Before he could answer, the satellite phone rang. Keller picked it up and heard the frazzled voice of a woman who identified herself as Graham's sister. He could hear ambulance sirens in the background.

"I only have a few minutes. I need to tell Jo her father is unconscious. I have an ambulance on the way and will call back when I know more. Can you get the message to her?"

"Yes, and I'll have her in the wheelhouse waiting for the return call." Keller hung the phone up and turned to Graham. "Go get Jo."

"What's going on?"

"Just. Get. Jo. Now!"

As Graham turned on his heels, Keller turned the boat. Full tanks and full wallets be damned. The only thing that was important now was getting Jo home.

CHAPTER FOURTEEN

Jo heard Graham calling out her name accompanied by his fast and heavy steps on the stairs. She turned just as he rounded the corner. "Something's wrong at home."

She pushed herself away from the table and followed Graham back up the steps. Her heart rose to her throat closing it off. In the wheelhouse, she tried to ask Keller for an update, but opening her mouth promised to open a floodgate of tears, so she clamped it shut.

Keller's face seemed to mirror the fear and pain thrumming through her. "You need to call your house. Right now. Graham's sister says there's an emergency."

"What's going on, Keller? Tell me, please!"

Graham said something was wrong. The punctuated timber of Keller's speech confirmed it was bad.

"I think it would be better if you got the information from someone who's there."

She picked up the phone, but then turned back to Keller. She wasn't sure why, but she didn't want the bad news from anyone but him.

Finally, he acquiesced. "All I know is that Faye found him unconscious and called an ambulance. It had just arrived while we were talking. She went to help them and said she'd call back, but I think you should call her."

Jo lifted a shaky hand to her mouth. She was unable to keep back a few stray tears that slid down her cheek. She let them fall unchecked and dialed the phone. "He seemed so good the other night," she whispered. To whom, she wasn't sure.

Faye's voice came across the line, and Jo could hear nothing but fear and panic.

"What's going on?"

"When you guys left, Graham asked me to come by and check on Lark now and again. He didn't come up to the diner for lunch as he has been, so I got worried. He didn't answer the door, and I had to climb in the window out front."

"Please! Just tell me what's wrong?"

"The paramedics said it looked like he overdosed himself on his insulin. He was passed out on the kitchen floor when I got here. I couldn't wake him, so I called 911."

"Was he still unconscious when they took him to the hospital?"

At her words, Graham's hands fell on her shoulders, squeezing them in support and she leaned back into him. Why was it whenever everything got to be too much, he was the one who was right there to hold her up?

This time, however, she didn't want the comfort of a friend. She wished Keller would offer his support.

"They gave him something in an IV."

"Dextrose?"

"Maybe. He was coming around when they were loading him in the ambulance. He was calling out for you and said he didn't want to go to the hospital, but the paramedics talked him into it."

"Thank heavens. Do you know what his sugar count was? Did the paramedics tell you?"

"No, they didn't. All I know is that after they checked it, they said he'd overdosed on insulin. I gave them the number to the boat. They said they'd have the doctor call you as soon as there was anything to tell you."

"Thanks, Faye. And thanks for just dropping by. You saved his life."

"Don't say that. He would have been all right."

"No." She swallowed hard. "He wouldn't have been without the IV."

"I'm going to head over the clinic and sit with him. I'll call you with an update."

"Thanks." Jo hung up the phone, and then spun on her heels away from Graham's touch. She leaned against the wall, but her legs gave way and she slid down until she was sitting on the floor.

"I've already pointed the boat for home. It's going to take all night but I'll get you in." Keller said, though he kept his eyes focused on the control panel and out the front window of the boat.

"No!" she spit out, trying hard to push the emotions down. "You're not loaded yet."

"But what if...you need to be with your father."

Keller putting her needs above his business touched her, but she knew in her heart the emergency had passed. "I really appreciate the thought, but it's not necessary. Thank heavens, Faye found him when she did, but he's got medical attention now. They'll even out his sugar and probably send him home in a couple of hours."

Graham sat down on the floor next to her. "I'm glad my sister went by tonight and found him too, but I don't think you should discount the seriousness of this. You should let Keller take you in."

"It's just not necessary," Jo said. "I've been dealing with his diabetes for a while now, and know how this works. I don't want you to burn extra fuel for nothing."

Keller spun his chair around so he could look at her. "To be honest, with this storm bearing down I was thinking about going in and offloading anyway."

"The tanks aren't full," she insisted.

"If I have to be held up because of the weather anyway, I might as well be productive. We can get the offload done. You can check on your dad. Who knows, you might have made enough money that you can take care of your debts and be done."

"I don't want you or any of the guys to lose money because of me." She balanced her elbows on her knees and buried her face in her hands.

Why can't anything be easy?

"It's my decision, and I've made it. We're headed in." Keller spoke firmly, decisively, as he gave his focus back to driving the boat. "Graham, head back down to the galley, get something to eat then hit the racks. I'm going to need someone to drive in a few hours so I can grab a short nap."

Jo and Graham both stood. He started down to the galley as she crossed to the chair opposite of Keller. "Do you mind if I sit up here and wait for the clinic or Faye to call?"

"Of course not. I like the company."

The company? Or my company?

Her thought process was jarred as Keller swore under his breath and turned the boat hard. The boat slammed against a large wave, and was thrown nearly vertical before it crashed hard against the water.

Jo was tossed from the seat, but grabbed the sill running along the wall and bent at the knees, a trick she'd learned on deck. She kept her center of gravity low, which helped her keep control of her body. She gripped the wood, but let her body sway with the force. When the natural rhythm of the sea returned, she pulled herself up straight. "You have nerves of steel."

He laughed. "No."

"You didn't even flinch. Just steered."

"Are you kidding? Stuff like that scares the crap out of me, but everyone's counting on me to keep the boat afloat and to get them home safe."

It hadn't taken her long to learn that Keller had a set of defensive walls that resembled hers. On the outside, he looked like the quintessential captain: strong, fearless, and maybe a little stupid. A guy would have to be dense or crazy to spend so much time battling Mother Nature to make a living.

In these quiet moments in his company, she'd learned a completely different man existed underneath those walls. He admitted fear and faced it with a humbleness, admitting his youth and inexperience, but accepting his responsibilities. There was an irony to that she found endearing.

As if she needed another reason to find him attractive.

The phone rang and Keller picked it up. After a brief exchange, he handed the phone to Jo.

"Faye, how's Dad?"

"There's good news and not-so-good news."

Jo couldn't understand why people felt the need to buffer bad with good, or camouflage it as not being as bad as it appeared. "Just tell me, please."

"They are getting his sugar in line. He's sitting up in bed and demanding to go home. Like normal."

"But..."

"The doctor wanted to check out his foot. Lark refused at first, which of course raised some suspicions."

The warnings given about losing a toe or even the foot at that last visit rolled through her mind. "How bad is it?"

"Sutherland is making arrangements to send him to the hospital up in Anchorage."

"When?"

"He would like to get him on the way immediately, but isn't sure that's possible with the storm rolling in. Lark needs to get some intense wound care or he could..."

"What?"

"Lose his foot, maybe even part of his leg. It looks awful, and smells worse. Didn't you have a nurse coming to check on him?"

Great question! She'd hired the woman her mom recommended because she trusted her mother, even paid the lady in advance. Had she failed, or had Lark refused the help. "When was the doctor going to call me?"

"As soon as transport was arranged."

"Okay. Thanks for filling me in. Have the doctor call me when he gets a chance and tell Dad I'm getting there as fast as I can."

"Of course." Then, an eerie silence. Jo would have thought Faye hung up if it wasn't for the static and her slow, deep breathing. "I think seeing you will be the best medicine he can get. He misses you."

Faye was probably right, but the comment stoked the fire of frustration that burned in Jo's chest. It'd been less than a week. What her Dad didn't seem to understand was enduring a short separation was worth the payoff. Or it would have been if he hadn't just ushered another bucket full of medical bills to their door. "Tell him I'm on the way."

After handing the phone back to Keller, he dropped it in the cradle without taking his gaze off the brewing seas. "How's Lark?"

She shrugged her shoulders and hopped back up into the opposite chair. "The crisis with his sugar has passed, but apparently he hasn't been taking care of his foot. The doctor is arranging transport to the hospital in Anchorage."

"That doesn't sound good."

"Why do I have to be there to take care of him? He's a grown man!" She felt guilty about venting her frustrations to her father's boss and friend, but she couldn't contain it.

"Lark's never seemed like the needy type to me."

"In most aspects of his life, he is one hundred percent self-sufficient. Tough as nails, like the rest of you guys."

"You guys?"

"Fishermen. The only exception to that whole persona is that he clings to his relationship with me. If I'm not at home every night—especially since he's gotten so sick—the world's coming to an end."

"He worries about you. That's just a father's way, I think."

"I get that. But I'm hardly a kid anymore. You should have seen how upset he was when I went to spend some time with my mom a couple of weeks ago."

"That's got to be hard, your parents being divorced."

She shrugged. "It's life, you know. I sensed I was different than the other kids in school, having to jump a plane to visit one parent or the other."

"If Lark didn't work on the boats, would you have spent more time with him in the winter?"

Could she tell him the truth? Why not? They seemed to bearing their souls in the privacy of the wheelhouse. "If he didn't fish, I don't think they would be divorced. I think there's a part of each of them that still loves the other, but distance is damaging to any relationship."

"Not everyone is suited for this way of life, or this job; and not everyone can be married to someone whose job takes them away from home. What's your mom's life like now?"

"Normal."

"What do you mean by that?"

Did he take offense?

That's what his tone would indicate. "My step-dad is a professor at a medical college, she's a nurse. They work during the day and come home at night to the house with the fenced-in yard and two point five kids."

"I guess that's one version of normal...in fairytale land."

Was he mocking her dream? The life she wanted more than anything, the life she felt cheated out of as a child. "It's not wrong to want stability!"

"Not at all, I just don't think it's realistic to think that so-called stable life will be free of pain or trouble. My mother made a marriage to a fisherman work. Other couples can't. But there are plenty of divorces in the land of picket fences too."

"But I think because he had to spend so much time on the boat, my dad over reacts and tries to over-protect. The way he was about me taking this job is a great example."

"Being out here isn't exactly summer camp. He knows the dangers."

"I get that, but how does not taking his medicine or refusing the care I arranged for him help? I'd hired someone to come over twice a day to assist him with his medications, clean his wound and change his bandages. If his foot's so bad after a week, I'm guessing he insulted and fired that woman the first day she tried to come."

A smirk turned Keller's lips. "Really? He seems so lovely and mild-mannered on the boat."

Heavy sarcasm laced his voice and Jo couldn't help but laugh. "I love him, but he frustrates me, especially when he does things like this to jeopardize his health."

"I'm going to give you a little take-it-or-leave-it advice. Don't waste a single moment being angry. Whatever the differences are between you, work them out. The last time I talked to my father I told him I didn't want to be anything like him." He paused, and swallowed hard. She could see his eyes getting glassy. "I regret that every day."

Seeing the raw emotion on his face touched Jo. In a way their spirits were kindred by the parental struggles. "I really am sorry about your father. I remember him to be so vibrant when he came into the cannery."

A smile briefly danced across his lips. "Vibrant. That's a good word. Loud and boisterous are two others that describe him."

"You must miss him horribly."

"I do. It's sort of weird when you think about it though. Not being there is normal in this business." He paused and Jo watched regret and sorrow wash over his face. "When I was growing up, he was never home. It wasn't just crab seasons; he was out after some kind of fish about forty weeks a year. He'd come home for a few days here and there, exhausted but bearing gifts. Those days would be a whirlwind of his exuberance for life. He'd take us out of school to do fun things, shower us with affection." A playful smirk chased the negative emotions off his face. "And nine months later we'd get a new baby brother or sister."

"How many siblings do you and Reese have?"

"Four sisters."

"Wow. I can't even imagine."

"You're an only child, right?"

She shook her head. "My mom has two kids with her second husband, a boy and a girl. They are a lot younger than me though: eight and eleven."

"So you grew up an only child."

She nodded, wasn't sure what to say to that, so she changed the subject. "When did you start fishing?"

"Part time when I was fifteen. I started going out on the boats during the summer when there was no school. I loved spending those long stretches of days and weeks with my father. He taught me everything I now know about fishing and running a boat."

"I sometimes wonder if my father would have ended up with his own boat if he hadn't had to take off summers to be with me. He sacrificed so much career-wise."

Keller shook his head. "Lark loves you. You're all he would ever talk about when we worked together on deck. I don't think my dad ever talked about his life at home when he was on the water."

"Isn't that some sort of code of the sea or something. I thought all fisherman locked their emotions up."

"That's what my last fight with Dad was about. Brie didn't want a never-there soon-to-be husband. She didn't want someone who was a thousand miles away when he was in the same room. And I wanted her, so I told him I was better than all of that. That I knew what family was about." He paused and scraped his hand along his jaw, "I was such an idiot."

"No. You were frustrated. I'm sure he knew you loved him."

"I stayed home that season, tried to fall in line at her uncle's freaking landscaping company, for what?"

"Brie?"

"Yeah...for Brie."

"You loved her?"

He shrugged his shoulders. "I thought I did at the time. Thought she loved me, but she kicked me out about three weeks after Dad's funeral. As soon as Reese and I figured out that the only way to put food on ours and Mom's table was to keep the boats on the water, she was done with me."

"That's pretty lousy." She didn't know what else to say, really wasn't even sure why he was telling her such personal stuff.

"Yeah. But that wasn't the point. Learn from my stupid mistakes and talk to your dad. Be there for him when he needs you. Nothing else really matters."

"Thanks, Keller." She felt like she should say more. She wanted to go to him, hug his neck. Offer him some comfort. But what was the point?

She wouldn't know his Brie if she bumped into her on the street, but somehow felt like they were a lot alike. Keller was a fisherman, cut from the same cloth her father and Graham were. Maybe the familiarity was why she felt so drawn to him, but what was it her father had told her?

Lust fades. Strong connections and friendships last. How would she ever be friends with someone who was never present? Keller had left the sea once, but its siren call had brought him back, even though he knew it would cost him Brie.

If his record showed her nothing else, it seemed a woman would never take priority in his life.

CHAPTER FIFTEEN

It didn't surprise Jo that the woman in the reception area and the nurse behind the counter greeted her by name. Not only was it a small town, but she'd spent more time in this clinic with her father in recent months than anyone should have.

As the nurse escorted her into the narrow hall between examining rooms, she said, "I'm going to put you in here. I know Dr. Sutherland wants to talk to you before you see your dad."

"When will they be moving him?"

"I just got word from the airport. The transport can leave within the hour. Sutherland has been here all night waiting for the storm to pass."

Jo paced the small room. Waiting sucked! She'd been doing it for twenty-seven hours now. Why couldn't the nurse just take her to her father?

A few moments later, the doctor came through the door, slipping into a white lab coat as he walked. His hair was tousled and exhaustion weighted his shoulders. "I'm glad you were able to make it in before we moved your dad. I know you'll both feel better that you got to see him."

"How's he doing? Is it really so bad that he needs to go to Anchorage?"

He pointed to a chair, taking a seat on the stool. "This infection in his foot has really taken hold. It's in his bloodstream now and may even be settling in the bone.

That's why his sugar's been hard to manage and spiking up and down on you."

"If you know what's wrong, why can't you treat it here?"

"That's what we've been trying to do for two months."

Jo shifted her weight in the chair as the familiar knots of frustration began tying up her shoulders. "He's so stubborn. If he'd only listened to you."

"Don't put this on him. The infection and the diabetes are feeding off each other. It's hard to control blood sugar counts when a body's fighting an infection, and the out-of-control sugar keeps his immune system from effectively fighting the bacteria. He needs to be on a very strong intravenous antibiotic, and constant monitoring. You know we don't have the facility or the staff here. I did give him a first dose overnight and stayed with him…"

"Thank you for that."

"I'm just glad this storm was a fast mover and we're able to get him on the way up there. Did you want to fly up with the transport? I can arrange it if you want."

"I don't know. Let me talk to Dad. It's going to be costly enough for him to go…"

"After he came back around last night, he sent Faye back to the house to get some medical assistance paperwork he'd been working on. One of the nurses helped him finish it and we got it submitted. I'm hoping that'll help you with the bills."

"That would be a relief." She paused, wrestled with all the emotions twisting her stomach, and then asked, "The intense treatment, it *will* clear the infection. Right?"

"I have no reason to think otherwise, but, I'm not so sure they'll be able to completely save his foot."

"What?"

"The flesh of one—maybe two—toes is looking pretty dead. If it were me, I'd suggest amputating them, but I'm going to leave that call up to the doctors in Anchorage."

How she'd hoped it wouldn't come to this. Her father's worst nightmare. "Can I see him now, please?"

"Of course."

* * * *

Standing in the hall outside her father's hospital room, Jo inhaled deeply and counted to ten as she let the breath escape her lungs in measured increments. Could she have prevented her father from getting this ill if she'd stayed home? Or had the woman she hired based on her mom's recommendation failed her?

The doctor had said it was the infection that was at the root of all his other problems, but she was having a hard time shaking off the veil of guilt that hung around her.

Gripping the door handle, she dug deep for the same strength she'd called on in the past week, and entered the room.

Lark was sitting up in the bed, sipping from a cup of coffee, and looked to be in good health. His youthful appearance and solid frame had a way of convincing most that he was still the man he'd always been, but Jo could see cracks in his armor. His dead-pan stare appeared shallow. He looked tired.

When he saw her, a smile tipped his lips. "You're home."

She sat on the edge of the bed, patted his hand and pushed the stray graying hairs off his forehead with her other hand—a not-so-nonchalant way of checking for a fever. "How are you feeling?"

"Fine now. Tell that snot-nosed doctor to cancel the transport. Now that you're home everything's going to be fine."

She shook her head. "I just talked to Dr. Sutherland. You're leaving for Anchorage within the hour. They're better equipped to treat your foot."

He waved his hand in front of his face. "But that's just not necessary."

Jo didn't know if he chose to be ignorant about his condition or really believed she had some magic touch that could cure everything. "What happened with the nurse I hired?"

"I swear I kept my promise to you. I ate only the meals she fixed, took the medicine she gave me, and stayed off my foot as much as possible. I've watched so many damn Andy Griffith reruns, I can probably recite them by heart. You know that's not me. I don't like to just sit."

"Thank you for doing that."

"It was awful, but the worst part is it didn't do any good."

"The doctor says it's the infection. This new medicine's supposed to help, but you need to be monitored closely." She paused, squeezed his hand a little tighter as she considered her next question. "Do you want me to come up there with you?"

"Of course I want you to, but it would just be too hard. They're telling me it will be at least a week, maybe two. What are you going to do? Stay in a hotel?"

"It would be very expensive. And besides fishing with Keller, I don't have a job right now."

"That fishing thing's over. Right? You go back to Mr. Crandell. He'll give you your job back. You are too good of an employee for him to let you go."

"I'm glad you think that, but I'm not so sure you're right. I'm guessing he's replaced me already." She stood and walked toward the door. What she had to say next would be harder for Lark to hear than it was for her to say. "As far as fishing, I might not be done. I did this to save the house. If I haven't earned enough, I may have to go back out."

Lark rolled his head away from her, his eyes shutting, obviously closing out her harsh words. She knew he was taking all of this as a personal hit to his ego, but they were out of time for him to cling to his chauvinistic ways. "I know you don't like being sick. You'd give anything to be out there working, but we have to play the cards we're dealt. Right?"

Lark returned his gaze to Jo, giving her a faint smile. "But if you've made enough to pay off the loan?"

She shrugged. "I won't know that until we're done offloading. Keller let me come check on you, but as soon as you're on the plane, I have to go help."

"How was the fishing? Did you get good numbers?"

She shrugged. "It was slow at first, but after a day or two it got a lot better. We came in a little early because of the storm."

"How about you? You holding up?"

"He says I'm doing a good job, as good as he'd expect out of any greenhorn. I didn't have a clue how hard the work was. And the cold—bitter, hellish cold.

And you and the other guys don't just do it for a week. You've done it year in and year out."

The look on Lark's face was hard to read. There was a sadness, but also a shine of pride.

"There's a lot of people—a lot of big, strong men—who crumble under the work. I've watched them come and go. It says something that you've hung with those guys once *and* want to go back out again."

"The last thing I ever want to do is go back out and fish crab. But if I haven't earned enough to pay off the mortgage, I will. You know why? Because you've worked your entire life to take care of me, and I'll be damned if you don't have that house to retire in. You deserve it."

"I don't know about all of that. I've done the best I could to get by and take care of you. No more, no less."

"And that's why I have to finish what I started. I just hope I'm strong enough to endure."

"Of course you are. You're my daughter."

She laughed. "That's right. And taking care of each other is what we do."

"I'm so angry at myself for letting this fall to you."

Jo knew it had taken a lot for her father to admit his perceived failing, and she leaned in. Wrapping her arms around his neck, she hugged him tight before whispering in his ear. "I want you to go up to Anchorage, listen to the doctors, and get well. When you get home, the house will be all ours."

* * * *

After Sutherland and the nurses loaded Lark into the ambulance to take him to the air transport, Jo turned back toward the docks. She pushed her hands into her pockets and lowered her head to shield her face from the cutting wind.

She'd walked three blocks before she allowed herself to feel the ache simmering in her heart. Through the fog of exhaustion, she realized how she and her dad had flipped roles. She was now a caregiver. And this moment resembled all of those falls of her youth, only in reverse.

He was headed off the islands on a plane, and she could very well be leaving again on a crab fishing boat. The way time passes enveloped her, freezing her feet to the snow-covered walk.

Looking up, she got her bearings and crossed the street, heading west until she hit the Elbow Room. She bellied up to the bar and fished her cell phone out of her pocket. Staring at the keyboard, she realized she didn't know the number she most wanted to dial, so instead called Graham.

When he answered his phone, she asked, "Is Keller there on deck?"

"He was, but I think he went to bed. What's wrong?"

"I need to talk to him."

"What is it? You can talk to me."

"Please, can you just ask Keller to meet me up at the Elbow room?"

After he agreed, she disconnected that call and dialed her mother.

CHAPTER SIXTEEN

Keller slammed the door of his truck and checked both directions before crossing the street.

He'd only just drifted off to sleep when Graham pounded on the door to the cabin and delivered Jo's message. Not sure what he'd find inside the bar, he opened the door with a bit of trepidation.

It wouldn't surprise him to see a crack in her façade. She'd rode an emotional roller coaster in the last twenty-four hours, with very little sleep.

Instead, he found her sitting alone, sipping a cup of coffee. He went to her, and took the stool next to her. "What's going on?"

"I got to visit with my dad before he left for Anchorage. The doctor is hopeful, but..." She braced her hands against the bar and looked down at her knees.

The need for business decorum faded, and Keller slid off the stool so he could move closer to her, wrapping an arm around her shoulder. "You need to go up to Anchorage. I can help you arrange a flight."

She curled to him, resting her hand on his hip bone. "No. Dad and I talked about it. I'm going to stay here and go out with you again if you'll let me."

"Of course. You did a top-notch job. You're always welcome on my crew." He didn't want to be separated from her, but did that make him selfish? "But if your dad needs you..."

She took a deep breath and inched back from him. "I called my mom and asked her to stay in touch with the doctors and decode all the medical speak to me."

"And she agreed."

"She's doing me one better. She's going to go to Anchorage to be with him and report to me from there."

To hear both Lark and Jo talk about her parents' less-than-cordial relationship, Keller never would have imagined Lark's ex would fly to his bedside. He'd taken notice of the woman when she was in the bar with Jo. She seemed out of place then and very different from either Jo or Lark. "That's really..."

"Surprising? I know. She said she's doing it for me."

Now, that made sense. Keller was well aware how hard it was for Jo to ask for help. The fact she had must not have been lost on her Mom. "That's great, but if you need to go, I understand."

She smiled at him, let her hand graze his arm. "Of course you do. I think that's why I called you. I know that more than anyone else, you know what I'm feeling right now."

Watching Jo wrestle to balance what she felt needed to be done with what she wanted to do was like stepping into some freaky time machine. The part of him that regretted lost moments with his dad wanted to put Jo in his truck and take her straight to the airport. His heart, however, argued loudly. Letting her slip away from him was just something he couldn't bear to do. Besides, he needed to respect Jo's feeling on this one.

His gut told him there was more to all of this than she was letting on, though. The strong woman he'd come to know hadn't wanted to leave the boat before the work was done and would have returned straight away if something wasn't really wrong. "I'm sorry you're going through this."

She nodded and stepped closer to him. "I shouldn't have pulled you away from the boat. I was on my way back to help with the offload when I froze up and called—"

Remembering what she'd told him before about gossip chains and small town chatter, he wondered if that's why she was holding something back now. "I'm glad you felt you could talk to me. You can tell me anything and it'll stay between us."

"I hated traveling back and forth to Fairbanks when I was a kid." The words spilled from her quickly, like some sordid secret she dare not whisper. "I was split right down the middle, didn't want to leave whichever of them I was with, and couldn't wait to see the other parent after so long of being away."

He appreciated she was opening a wound on her soul, but wasn't sure why, in this moment, she felt like it had to come off her chest. "I can see how that would be hard."

"You know, all my friends would talk about the life they someday wanted: the kind of guy they wanted to marry, the things they would do before they settled down, and where they wanted to go to college. They had all these wild, fantastic dreams full of adventure, and all I wanted was to settle down. I didn't want to have to travel anymore. I wanted to know that tomorrow night I would be sleeping in the same bed as I was in that moment."

"Is there something standing in your way of that?"

She turned to face him, gave him her full attention. Maybe *he* was the one standing in her way. That didn't make sense. She thought of him as a means to an end, a catalyst to get the money she needed.

Or did she feel more?

After what seemed like a long moment, she said, "When I was walking back toward the docks, I realized that it all might be slipping through my fingers, that I might not ever have the one thing that always mattered the most."

"The house?"

She cradled the cup in her hands, staring at its contents, making him believe that wasn't it.

"Your father *is* going to be all right. Isn't he?"

She nodded, and then slowly turned back to him. "I was being stupid. Just a panic attack. I shouldn't have called you out."

"If you needed to talk to someone, I'm glad you turned to me." He felt like she was still holding back, didn't really believe she'd fell victim to anxiety. Sure, everyone has their breaking point and she'd been put through the wringer this past week, but it just didn't fit into her character.

But, he couldn't push it. She'd turned to him, and when she was ready to really talk, he wanted her to come to him again.

"There's something I wanted to talk to you about anyway," Keller said as he reached into the back pocket of his jeans and brought out the crumpled pieces of paper he'd found in the bait freezer. "You did this?"

She looked at the page and her scribbled notes. "You said to keep track of bait usage and let you know where we stood."

"And you did a great job of that, but this." He pointed to the scribbling of a formula that had confused him. "You were trying to figure something else out."

"I tried to use math as a distraction. I started to wonder if there was a correlation between the amount of bait or the mixture of the bait and the yield of crab. Of course there were too many unknown variables, but it kept my mind off the cold and the pain."

"When did you have the time to do all this?"

She shrugged "I did most of it in my head while I was filling bait cans or helping to sort crab. Then, when I'd get a few minutes between strings, I'd write it down. It's not really a big deal."

"For me it is." He'd mentioned to her before that the business was struggling, but wasn't sure he wanted her to know just how much. Now wasn't the time to let pride get in the way. She had a strength that countered his weakness. "Would you be willing to help me?"

"After everything you've done for me? Of course. What do you need?"

"Would you look through my books, see if you can help me figure out how to increase my profits?"

"Sure." She paused, tapped her fingers against the bar before continuing. "Why don't you come over to my house after we're done on the boat? I'll make dinner."

"Perfect."

But was it?

He was having a hard enough time not following through on his desires with her when they were on the boat and surrounded by the other men. How would he keep their relationship professional in the privacy of her home?

* * * *

Keller paused on the doorstep of the house and took a minute to get his bearings. After the offload and a long nap, he'd taken a shower and then stopped at the market to buy dessert and a bottle of wine.

Maybe he'd misinterpreted her invitation. She probably wanted to do this at her house so she could avoid Pete and the crew, and had offered to make dinner because it was the polite thing to do.

It wasn't a date, and he'd been a fool to treat it as one.

He pushed the doorbell anyway.

Dessert and wine don't make it a date, he reassured himself. *It's just good manners to bring something when you were invited over. Right?*

The door opened and Jo greeted him warmly. "You made it!"

She was wearing black knit pants that hugged her legs, much like the ones she'd worn that night in the bar when this whole thing had started. Tonight the leggings were covered with a light, loose, blouse that was a swirl of black, red, and deep blues. Her hair that normally fell in straight lines over her shoulder had big full curls framing her face.

She must have enjoyed some pampering time after the long, hard week on the boat. Or had he misjudged her?

Did *she* view the evening as something more too?

Suddenly, he was happy to have spent the extra time on his appearance and the amenities. He stepped into the foyer, offering the brown paper bag with the grocery's logo. "I can't thank you enough for doing this for me."

She took the bag and curiously peeked in. "You didn't have to bring anything."

"Nonsense. My momma raised me right." He noticed the dimple in her left cheek and wished she'd smile more often. He knew why she didn't, was well familiar with the emotions darkening her mood, and was grateful he'd been able to lighten it, if only a bit.

She slid the plastic case out of the bag. "Chocolate and raspberry cheesecake? You *do* know what a woman likes."

"I'm sure it's not as good as mine. Had I been home, in my kitchen, I'd have made one from scratch."

"You bake?"

"It's better than starving."

She laughed and motioned him to follow her into the kitchen. "Well, I can fix enough meals to stay alive too, but I don't think I'd try to make a cheesecake."

After she set the package and the bottle of wine on the table, she gave her full attention to him again.

"I rarely get the time, but I do enjoy it." He motioned to the briefcase in his hand. "Where do you want me to put this?"

"Just set it down anywhere. I'll have a look after dinner." She turned to the stove and opened the oven, pulling out the casserole. "Dinner's ready if you want to take a seat. I hope you don't mind. I went for simple, and like I said, I eat to survive."

"I'm sure it's great." He sat at the table, feeling a flush warm his face. He wanted to believe he was sweating because the oven had overheated the kitchen, but knew that wasn't the case. It was Jo, and had been since that night in the bar.

The next half-hour was spent grazing over the dinner and sipping on the wine while they shared stories of their families. Keller regaled her with many tales of growing up with five siblings.

Jo seemed just as intrigued by the large family experience as he was with her solitary youth. He enjoyed hearing about her lone flights between her parents' houses, though he sensed she worked hard to describe them as huge adventures to disguise how lonely her childhood had been.

He always believed he'd been raised to be strong and independent, but it was in a very different way than she'd been. Keller always knew if he miss-stepped or needed help, someone in his family would be close by to lend a hand. Jo had her parents, but her mom and dad barely spoke to each other, often putting her in the middle. She had to be more self-sufficient than he ever had to be.

But at what cost?

When they were done eating, he cleared the dishes and put away the leftovers while she began sorting out the mess that was his accounting system. After flipping through his battered and worn ledger for a few moments, she disappeared and returned with a laptop. Within minutes, she was putting his data into a spreadsheet and running formulas to decipher it.

He refilled their wine glasses and dropped down to the chair next to Jo, watching as she ran her fingers down the last column of numbers in the ledger.

A cursory look told him his math wasn't far off, but it was some of the more complicated sheets she flipped to on the screen that he couldn't make heads nor tails of.

"Is this the same way your father kept records. In a print ledger?"

"Yes. Honestly, it never occurred to me to do something different. Before eighteen months ago, all I had to focus on was my job on deck."

"You don't give yourself enough credit."

A tired exhale escaped from him. "Reese and I had begun training to become captains, about six months before his heart attack. A good thing, we'd never had been able to get our licenses so fast if we hadn't."

"Even after you quit fishing, you still trained?"

He shook his head. "But you have to realize it was only a couple weeks between my blowout with Dad and his death. And maybe two more weeks before I knew what needed to be done and got my ass back in classes."

Jo's eyes darkened and he guessed she was drawing a parallel between his relationship with his father and her situation with Lark. Not wanting to put a dark cloud on what had been a nice evening, he said, "Being a captain's more than knowing where the fish are or leading the crew. I had to learn the ins and outs of the boat, how everything functions mechanically, and making the business side profitable. *That's* where I've really failed."

Her lower lip curved up between her teeth and she turned back to the computer. She clicked a few buttons and he could hear a printer in the other room kick into gear.

Jo left and came back just a moment later with the pages. "You're keeping your head above water."

"Barely. Do you know the profit on the first trip yet?"

She leaned over his shoulder and guided him to the third page, and then pointed to a box toward the bottom of it.

"Damn!" He leaned his elbow against the table and used that hand to rub the back of his neck.

"Is that bad? You're in the black."

He didn't look up at her, only turned his attention back to the paper. "It's okay, not great. I need great. We still have a lot of work to do."

Keller had told her she could continue working, but after the last week on the boat, she was really hoping to be done and out. "I haven't earned enough yet, have I?"

He picked up the calculator out of the open briefcase resting on the table and started punching numbers in. "You're at about three grand. It's a sliding scale, though. Each trip should be more profitable than the one before it. It's why it benefits everyone if I cut checks at the end of the season."

"Three is not enough." She lowered herself back to her chair, but sat on it sideways, so she was turned toward him.

A piece of him was glad that she might continue on the boat, but guilt for finding joy in her pain quickly shadowed it. He laid a hand on hers. "You've never told me how much you need."

CHAPTER SEVENTEEN

Jo took a deep breath, and fought the urge to tell Keller everything, even though her father wouldn't want anyone to know how much he owed on the house. She hadn't even told Mr. Crandell and she'd known him a whole lot longer than Keller.

Somehow, she felt closer to him, though, and he'd put his butt on the line for her. "Eighteen grand."

He leaned back in the chair. "It's possible for you to earn that much, but not in one trip. If you want to hit that goal, you'll have to continue on the boat."

The muscles in her shoulders loosened a bit more. She'd expected another offer for a loan. Instead, Keller had respected how she felt and trusted her ability to handle the situation and the job. "Are you sure you want to take me out again?"

"Of course. I told you in the bar that you've proven yourself to me. You have a place on my boat for the rest of the season, longer if you want it."

"I do...but..." Even though her mom was jetting to be by her father's side and make medical decisions in her place, it still felt wrong to leave.

"Your father?"

"Part of me wants to be up in Anchorage with him, but there's nothing I can do there, and going just creates more bills."

The look on Keller's face—a mixture of concern and empathy—gave her a little comfort. He slid to the edge of his chair and laid a hand on her forearm first. When she didn't resist his touch, his hand slithered up to her shoulder and wrapped around her back.

Her initial urge was to pull back. Giving in to her desire would only complicate their relationship. Instead, she collapsed to him, hugging his neck. Her fight dissolved, the need to touch Keller—and be touched by him—won out.

"I'm so sorry," Keller said. "He's sicker than any of us really know. Isn't he?"

She inched herself back, sitting up, but let her hand graze down his arm. "He's lived hard and done a lot of damage to his body. He's stable right now, and the doctor believes that the hospital in Anchorage will be able to clear up his infection. The next few weeks will be hard on him. That's why it's so important that I succeed. As much as I want to go up there, I need to be on the boat. Thank you, for letting me go back out."

"There's no reason to thank me. You worked hard for your spot. You deserve it. You're amazing."

Amazing. Exactly how she felt about him. He'd provided this delightful mix of being strong without making her feel weak in his presence. He'd quickly become someone she could turn to. At times, she believed he felt the same way, at other times, she wasn't so sure.

Keller twisted his fingers. He seemed to be trying to muster up the courage to ask her something. So, she held her tongue and waited, hoping he would find his words.

"Is there any truth to what your father says? That you and Graham are destined to be together?"

She rolled her eyes and shook her head. "Graham is more like a brother to me than a friend. We grew up together."

"Is there anyone?"

She looked into his eyes, wishing she had some super power and could read his mind. Was he testing the ground? Did he have similar feelings for her that she had developed for him? Could it be? "That I have romantic feelings about?"

"Yes."

She could hear a little hitch in Keller's breath and see the anticipation on his face. Still, it had to be one of those things that was just too good to be true.

"I haven't been in a relationship or dated anyone for several months. But there is someone who's caught my eye recently."

"There is?"

"I haven't known him for very long." She looked away, dug down to find the strength to continue. Of everything she'd had to do in the past week, *this* was the hardest of them all. She twirled her finger in the large curl brushing the side of her face and committed to following through. "It's complicated. He's sort of my boss."

Keller couldn't stop the smile that turned his lips. The playful, slow tease seemed less painful now that he knew they were on the same page. "I have it on good authority that he's interested in you too."

She opened her mouth to speak but emotion and stress balled in her throat, impeding the words.

Now what?

He touched the strand of hair she'd been playing with, and pushed it off her face. "Please, Jo. Say something."

"Really? You mean it?"

"Yes. Since that night in the bar. All I've been able to think about is kissing you."

"So, why haven't you?"

"I'm not sure—"

The reasons didn't matter. Jo slid to the edge of the chair, tossed her arms over his shoulders and pressed her lips to his. The movement must have taken him by surprise, because his body tensed ever-so-briefly, before he leaned into her kiss. The taste of the wine on his lips made her head light.

He enveloped her in his embrace, gliding his hands up her spine, and beneath her hair. Their tongues entwined, and he pulled her closer, but not close enough for her.

Apparently not close enough for him either. He stood, guiding her up, pulling their bodies tighter.

The kiss came to a natural end, and she nibbled at his chin, softly giggling. "I've wanted to do that for so long."

Keller pressed his forehead to hers and then brushed his soft lips against her temple. "Me too."

He guided his other hand along the edge of her neck, tracing the line of her jaw, and lifting her gaze to his. "You're probably the most capable person I've ever met. I know you can take care of yourself and your father all on your own. I just want you to know that you don't have to."

The idea that he was willing to stand by her, and support her, not because she was weak or needed his help, but because he just wanted to be there for her was enough to push away the baggage she'd been carrying. Jo danced her fingers up through his hair and steered his mouth back to hers.

His hands clawed at her back and those silk-soft lips pressed tightly to hers. As rough and tough as he was in every other way, it amazed her how tender he was in this moment. That professional wall they'd worked painstakingly to maintain, crumbled. There was no fighting it now. They'd crossed this line, and there was no going back.

As the kiss broke, he slid his fingertips down her spine sending a shiver to her very core. "What do you say we take the wine and go in the other room?"

Jo nodded, grabbing the bottle as he picked up the two glasses, gripping both stems between separate fingers of the same hand.

In the living room, he guided her toward the couch, but she gave his arm a tug, bringing his attention back around. When his eyes met hers, she tossed her head down the hall and then spun on her heels, leading him toward her bedroom.

She flipped on the lamp, but the dull, bluish light barely illuminated the room. This was her space. Yes, it was small and functional with only the furniture she needed, but it was her haven, and the place she wanted to share with Keller.

Jo sat on the edge of the bed, placing her hands on the mattress directly behind her, and leaning back. "Am I moving too fast?"

He placed one knee to the mattress next to her hip, and lowered his body, forcing her to lay further back on the bed. "Am I?"

She pressed a hand to his stomach, inching his body

up just enough that she could reach the drawer on the nightstand. Once open, she pulled out a ribbon of red foil wrappers. "I went shopping this afternoon too."

Keller picked up the condoms and tore away one of them, tossing one to the bed and dropping the rest back in the drawer.

Definitely fast! But, the tension that had been passing between them all week had reached its boiling-over point. That kiss had been like taking the plug out of the dam.

Flat on her back, she reached for the trim at the bottom of his sweater, lifting it away from his body. "I want to be closer to you."

She wasn't used to the desperation in her voice, or the desire burning within her. Even when she was begging for a spot on his boat, she'd done her best to come from a place of strength, had never wanted to show the vulnerability she now displayed. But, this was Keller.

Her harbor in the storm.

He pulled back to look in her eyes, and she took the opportunity to lean up enough to pull the light-weight blouse over her head, exposing a black lacy bra.

She tossed the shirt toward the floor and reached for him again.

The distance between them closed and he slid a hand beneath her, lowering his mouth to the delicate flesh where her neck sloped into her shoulder. His tongue slid against the bone.

"You're wearing too many clothes."

He stopped kissing her flesh long enough to chuckle. "What's your hurry?"

"No rush. Just want to—need to—feel you close."

His mouth slid down, his tongue flickering against the line of her bra, while his hands groped their way to her hips. Lifting them off the bed, he pulled her pants down as he brought himself to his feet again.

Gripping her foot, he raised her leg and flicked his tongue against the inside of her ankle.

She couldn't stop the soft giggle that erupted, didn't want to contain the sheer joy she felt.

As he tugged, she wiggled on the bed and her pants and tiny black underwear slipped from her body, joining her blouse in a heap on the floor.

"You're so beautiful." His words sounded corny, but she could see a sincerity in his eyes. He wouldn't lie to her, or put on airs.

"You're still dressed." Her voice sounded like a whimper and reflected the pent-up need rising inside her. She withered again on the bed when he nibbled at the soft flesh of her calf. She laughed and submitted to his teasing, while reaching behind her and releasing her bra, sending it to join the rest of her clothes.

"You are so impatient." He stepped between her legs, and rested his hands on her hips, positioning her at the edge of the bed. Leaning over her, he pressed his mouth to just above her belly button, slithering his tongue against her stomach as he worked his sweater up over his shoulders. He only broke contact with her long enough to pull the sweater the rest of the way off.

She brought his hand to her mouth, sliding his index finger against her lips in anticipation. "No more teasing. I don't think I can take it."

"I'm only just getting started with you." He snaked his other hand up her calf to the inside of her thigh. With a gentle touch, he spread her legs further, opening her up for his own display. After a painful pause, he continued moving his fingers up until they found her most intimate spot.

Jo's hips lifted off the bed, prodding him to continue his manipulations. She couldn't stop the guttural moan as she slid her hands down over her breast bone and stomach reaching for him. "Still too many clothes."

He stepped out of his shoes while unbuttoning and unzipping his jeans. As he struggled to get out of them, she laughed.

Keller nearly tripped over his own feet. Jo knew that he had a great sense of balance after all the time he'd spent on deck, and could only blame the urgency of the moment for making him clumsy.

She wiggled from beneath his touch, finding the condom he tossed down earlier. Moving to the center of the bed, she made room for him to lay next to her.

He obliged, and wrapped her up in his embrace, pulling her close so that he could kiss her again.

His hands slid down her back, beneath her hair, groping the flesh of bottom. Having ripped open the foil packaging and tossed it in the direction of their clothes. Reaching between them, she explored his body and stroked him to full arousal.

Keller rolled her to her back, coming down on top of her.

Too many sensations assailed her: the weight of his body, the feel of his skin against hers, the musk scent of his arousal. She gripped at his shoulders, holding on to him as if her life depended on it and wondering how she ever got along without him before.

"This means something to me," he whispered. "You mean something to me. I want you to know that."

"For me too."

"Are you sure you want to do this?"

"I'm positive. I'm not a white knight kind-of-girl. You're the first guy who's gotten that about me. You've given me your trust and the room to do what I needed to. And, showed me I don't have to face my problems alone."

He'd been supporting his weight on his arms, but with her words, he let his body drop to hers, and she welcomed him. His hot breath brushed her cheek before his mouth captured hers. His tongue explored her mouth and she wrapped her legs around his hips moaning as his pelvis rocked against hers.

Pressing against the small of her back, he lifted her hips, giving him more intimate access. He dropped his body again, and pushed himself inside her.

She shuddered as he entered her and she gasped his name, gripping his body tighter.

Keller glided against her, and she nestled her cheek in the crook of his neck, kissing away the sweet-salt moisture beading there. She met each thrust, the soft and smooth rocking pushing her closer to release.

Within the confines of her room, in his arms, the rest of the world faded away.

Maybe he wasn't like her father, Graham or the other fishermen she knew. He had left the sea behind once. Maybe, for her, he'd do it again.

CHAPTER EIGHTEEN

Keller's eyes fluttered before opening. He tightened his embrace around Jo. Her head now rested on his shoulder and her arm was draped across his abdomen. The night had been a blur, episodes of passion over and again, separated by brief periods of rest.

It had been well worth the wait, but the reasons why he'd resisted the attraction eluded him now.

Ledgers and crab count, and profit and loss were off in the foggy distance. Allowing himself to feel everything he'd worked so hard to hold at bay, sparked a hope. Maybe life didn't have to be solitary. Maybe she was the ultimate catch, a woman who was strong enough to stand by him, even when he had to be away.

Keller's fingers danced against Jo's shoulder, twisting in her hair. "You feel so good."

"I don't ever want to leave this bed."

"Me either." He squinted through hooded eyes at his extended arm, focusing in on his watch. It was later than he thought. "But I should probably get to the boat."

"What about breakfast?"

He tightened his embrace and leaned in, nibbling on her ear. "You're enough for me."

She squirmed and giggled.

He'd never grow tired of the sound of her laugh.

"Seriously!"

He pushed against the mattress, sliding up the headboard, and she turned to sit next to him. "I'll grab something on the way. How about you?"

"Do I have time to take a shower and call my mom before I come down?"

"Of course. We won't push off for a few hours." He draped his arm over her shoulder, and she leaned into him again. He kissed her forehead, and searched for the words to broach the touchy subject that was worrying him. "I'm not ashamed of what we did. You have to know that. I don't care who knows about—"

"But you don't think we should be open about *this* on the boat."

The concern, heavy as an anchor, lifted from his chest. He should have known she'd understand. "I just don't want the guys—"

"To think the only reason you want me back on the boat is—"

"Because we both know that's not true." He slid his hand under her chin, guiding her gaze to his. "Are you okay with that?"

"Yeah. Pete would make my life hell."

Keller slid a finger along her hair line and then traced the edge of her jaw. "It's going to be hard to go back to hiding my feelings."

She kissed the palm of his hand. "Then we need to hurry up and get out there." She slid her tongue along the length of his finger. "And catch the crab," She paused to kiss the inside of his wrist. "So we can get back here."

Keller groaned and guided her up so he could cover her mouth with his again. "I like this motivation."

* * * *

Keller boarded the boat, surprised at how alive he felt given his lack of sleep. The hours spent in port during offloads were usually used to catch up on the missed slumber, but being with Jo had been more rejuvenating. It showed him just how much he'd shut down since Brie left.

The rest of the crew was prepping the deck for departure. Fred and Norm were checking in the bait delivery, while Graham and Pete examined the stack. Keller paused at the door to the cabin and called out, "We're pushing off in three hours."

Inside the galley, he poured himself a cup of coffee and grabbed a doughnut from the box on the counter. Balancing the sustenance in one hand and his briefcase in the other, he headed for the stairs to the wheelhouse.

"Can we talk for a minute?"

Seeing Graham in the galley doorway, Keller turned, set his briefcase down, and slid into the booth. "What's on your mind?"

Graham shifted his weight from one hip to the other. "I drove by Jo's this morning to check on her and Lark before we left port."

The look on Graham's face spoke loud and clear. He'd seen Keller's truck in her driveway. Jo had assured him there was nothing but friendship between Graham and her, but obviously her buddy hadn't got the memo. "And..."

"What are you doing? She doesn't need complications in her life."

"There's no reason to go all big brother here."

"She obviously needs me to protect her from you. After everything she's been through, she doesn't need you playing with her."

Keller pushed himself to his feet. "Who says I'm playing?"

Clenched tight fists bounced against Graham's thighs and he looked as if he was ready to pounce. "You spent the night with her! Now she's going to fly up to Anchorage to be with Lark and we're going back out. And you'll see her... when?"

"Lark was moved up to Anchorage yesterday, and Jo is going back out with us. She'll be here soon."

"I thought it was for only one trip! Besides, Lark needs her."

"They both decided it would be better if she didn't go. Jo's mom is going to check on his care and report to Jo."

"That doesn't mean she has to come back out—"

"She wants to work and she earned the spot."

Graham stepped closer, invading Keller's personal bubble. "This isn't the fucking Love Boat. You know that better than anyone else."

Keller wasn't about to be intimidated. He was beginning to suspect that Graham had feelings Jo wasn't aware of, but she'd made it clear how she felt. He stepped forward. "Jo's place on this boat is hers for as long as she wants it, and that's because she did her job better than I could have ever hoped. What goes on between us is just that. None of your business."

Keller spun on his heel grabbing his coffee and his briefcase.

Graham spoke to his back. "You're selfish. You don't care if she gets hurt or not."

Keller turned back. "Me? What about you? You don't care what she feels like or what she wants. Only what you want for her or what you think she should be doing."

Graham didn't respond, only turned and slammed the cabin door, Keller continued his trek up to the wheelhouse, trying to shake off the argument with Graham. He picked up his clipboard, and scanned his to-do list before he called the *Melbourne* and collected the data from their first offload.

He'd no sooner hung up, when his phone rang again. Caller ID told him it was his mother.

"How's everything going?"

Keller hadn't stopped smiling since he'd woken up in Jo's arms, even Graham's little outburst had only distracted him briefly, but to hear his mother's voice lifted him even higher. "I can't complain. We've finished the first offload for both boats yesterday and are getting ready to head back out. The numbers could have been better, but there's no reason to grumble. How's everything there?"

"Well...that's why I'm calling."

For the first time, Keller noticed the normal cheerful lilt to his mother's voice was missing. "What's wrong?"

"Reese had to take Carol back to the hospital this morning. Her labor started again. I don't know anything else yet."

Keller wasn't sure what to say and took a minute to contemplate. Jumping a plane for home would mean no crab in the tank, no money for his crew, and no bills paid. It would be the final blow to the company, and to Jo. She couldn't save her father's house without another trip...or two. Still, this was family. "Should I come home?"

"No. Reese was adamant about that. He wanted me to let you know what was going on, but insisted there was no reason to panic."

"Are you sure?"

"Me? No. But your brother is right. The doctors have stopped labor once, there's no reason to think they can't get it under control again."

"Okay." He exhaled, it was the answer he'd wanted to hear, but it didn't stop the wave of guilt from crashing in on him. Memories of his father being in critical condition and him being so far away nudged him to go, despite what he'd been told. "The very first sign that things are heading south, you'll call?"

"Of course. But I think Reese is right. We should all maintain business as usual until we have a good reason to change course."

"Between you and me, do you think there's going to be a reason?"

There was a long silence. She spoke again just as Keller began to think he might have lost the connection. "It's possible you'll have to come home on a moment's notice."

"Okay, Mom. I'll keep that in mind." Out the front window he saw Jo make the jump from dock to boat and felt a tightening low in his gut. He struggled against the desire to descend the steps and greet her with a hug. "I need to go get ready to head out. I'll talk to you soon."

CHAPTER NINETEEN

Jo climbed the steps to the wheelhouse, handed Keller one of the cups of coffee she was carrying and sipped from the other. She then dialed her mother's number on the satellite phone.

Somewhere along the line, everything had fallen into place and had become routine. Even the sore muscles and upset stomach felt like it was just part of everyday life. With the ringing in her ear, she was able to balance the phone on her shoulder and wrap a free arm around Keller's neck and lean her head against his. Stolen moments like these were rare, but when they happened, she was compelled to take advantage of them.

He tipped his head down and kissed her arm.

"Mom," she greeted. "How's everything there?"

"It's going well. I told you I'd call if anything changed."

Her mother didn't sound well, she sounded stressed. "I know, but I wanted to check in with both of you."

"You do realize it's the middle of the night."

The sea water had left her watch inoperable and the long shifts and little sleep had altered her internal clock. She just assumed because she was up, everyone was. "I didn't. I'm sorry."

She could hear rustling and could imagine her mother stirring in the bed. "No. It's okay. I shouldn't be cranky with you. I was afraid, given the hour, that it was the hospital."

"You told me he's been doing really well with the new antibiotics. Why would the hospital be calling you in the middle of the night?"

"When you've been in the medical field as long as I have, you know things can change at a moment's notice. He's fine. I promise. Now, if you have time in four or five hours, why don't you call over to the hospital and talk to him. He would like that."

"I'll make time." Jo paused, couldn't shake the feeling that something wasn't right with her mother. Then again, it was the middle of the night and Jo had been calling her three times a day. Maybe entrusting her mother to her father's care meant giving Elle some latitude.

After chatting for a few more minutes, Jo hung up the phone and moved around so that she could kiss Keller's cheek.

"Everything okay?" he asked.

"Mom says so, but I don't know. She sounded funny."

"It *is* the middle of the night."

She nudged his shoulder. "Why didn't you tell me that before I dialed the phone?"

"I figured you knew!" He reached up, sliding his hand behind her neck and pulling her down so he could kiss her mouth. "Be extra careful out there. The weather has really picked up."

* * * *

The ship tossed high again and Jo bent at the knees and braced her hands straight out as she slid across the deck, not prepared for the force her elbows would take when she hit the sorting table. The instinct to shake out her arms was ignored and she instead covered her head just before the wave washed over the deck and drenched her with the ice cold water.

It had been three days of this: grinding the same routine repeatedly for long, long stretches before being granted a few hours of sleep, and a few stolen moments in Keller's embrace while the rest of the crew slept.

The weather had grown increasingly worse, with today being the nastiest she'd experienced in all of her time on deck.

Graham's arm looped through her shoulder bringing her to her feet. "Are you all right?"

"I'm fine. I'm fine."

"Stay on your feet. You know this!" He screamed to be heard, or maybe it was more about his irritation. Keller had told her about how Graham had confronted him about the night they'd spent together, and Graham had been chilly with her this whole trip.

She pushed past him getting back to her position. "Don't act like *you* weren't sliding across the deck on your ass too."

"Your father will skin me alive if I don't make sure you land on dry ground."

"Don't worry about me. I'm doing fine."

The routine continued, and soon another pot was locked on the launcher. She pitched herself in, switched out the bait strings and slid out with a fluidity that could only come from the hundreds of times she repeated the motion.

"Good job," Graham mumbled.

An apology for the harsh remarks he's made?

"Would you two lovebirds save the foreplay for when you're back in your bunks," Pete interrupted.

Against her inner nature, Jo bit her tongue and helped sort the crab, not giving Pete the satisfaction of even a glare.

"You're an asshole, you know that." Apparently Graham had reached his breaking point and was through being Jo's silent protector.

"I just want a little peace on deck. The weather sucks and I'd like to focus on getting the job done so we can head for town and offload your little bad-luck-charm."

"Who says I'm done after this trip?" Jo stood tall and challenged Pete, even though she was praying the bounty from the two trips would be enough to pay off the mortgage. "Keller says I have this job for as long as I want it."

"Only one reason I can think of as to why he'd say that. What does your fiancé here think about you spreading your legs for ol' Kell?"

Had she and Keller not been successful in their attempts to hide their budding relationship, or had Graham not kept silent? Still, she was prepared to lunge across the table, if necessary, to shut Pete's mouth. Graham was one step ahead of her.

He grabbed Pete's shoulder and twisted them so they were face to face. "Never! Ever! Talk about her like that."

Pete pushed Graham off him, yelling, "Get the fuck away from me."

"Knock it off!" Keller's voice came over the speakers. "I don't care what's going on, but it needs to stop! Now! We're coming up on the next pot."

Jo picked up the used bait strings and started for the bait table. She'd just picked up two fresh setups when the boat tossed sharply to the right. She grabbed the edge of the table and held on for dear life as her legs were washed out from under her.

A loud siren went off and Fred yelled, "Man overboard!"

Jo pulled her feet beneath her body and hopped up. She headed for the rail, scanning the deck and taking inventory of the crew.

Where's Pete? Pete was missing.

An extreme nausea bubbled up from her gut. This time guilt was the cause instead of the tossing seas. How many times had she wished he would just go away?

But not like this.

The boat tipped sharply again, this time from Keller turning them back around. "Jo, get away from the rail! Where's Pete! Someone get a lock on him!" Keller's voice cut through the icy air, and the panic sent a chill down her spine. Keller didn't overreact. His panic proved that this was off-the-scales catastrophic.

"Where is he?" Graham's voice cut the air.

"I can't see him!" Norm responded. He circled his hand above his head. "Keep turning Keller! We can't find him!"

Ignoring Keller's order to abandon the rail, Jo pushed her way forward and scanned the water. In the distance she saw Pete, waving his arms above his head, before sinking below the surface. "I got him! Right there!" She pointed to the spot he'd disappeared from, just as he popped up above the waves again.

"I see him," Keller responded. "Good work, Jo! Who's got the ring? Let's get him a line!"

Graham's arm came across her chest, pushing her back. He locked his focus and twisted his body to the right, the life preserver like a Frisbee in his arms.

Jo could see the weight of another man's life heavy on his shoulders. He snapped back and tossed the ring. She couldn't see through the wall of deck hands, but heard a resounding cheer, telling her Graham's shot had hit its mark.

"Norm and Graham, as soon as he clears the deck get him in here and get those wet clothes off him. Jo and Fred secure the deck and hold."

After giving her captain a thumbs up, she stepped back out of the way as the two chosen deck mates helped Pete over the rail with the help of the crane. His frosty stare met hers and she could feel blades of contempt being stabbed at her. His skin ashen and his lips blue, Jo knew one thing for sure, Pete had just cheated the grim reaper out of his bounty.

Graham and Norm each slid an arm under one of his shoulders and carried him from the deck.

She'd heard her father say it repeatedly. Keller and Graham had tried to warn her, too. Now, she'd seen it with her own eyes and felt the fear twisting her gut.

This job was lethal.

If she had been standing where Pete was when the boat pitched, it very well could have been her in the water.

Fred came up behind her and squeezed her shoulders. "You did good, Jo. Another thirty seconds in that water and he'd be dead."

She cast off his touch and moved to the table. Following Keller's orders, she made sure it was secure before checking the block. "I didn't have anything to do with getting him out of the water."

"You're the one who found him. That was probably his last time breaking the surface."

But, was it her fault to begin with. Had she distracted Pete? Had Graham's fight in her honor somehow led to it? "I'm glad I could help, but you know, maybe Pete's right. Maybe I'm just a big, dark cloud over this boat."

Fred followed her across the deck, grabbed her arm, and spun her to him. "Pete's not right. Okay, Pete's an asshole. This boat needs a fifth deckhand, and as far as I'm concerned that's you this season. I know your dad's not doing well and you want to be with him, but we need you too."

"I don't know."

"I do know. And I'll tell it to Keller too."

Jo was at a loss for words. Fred's praise had tightened her throat. It was one thing to be appreciated for how hard she'd worked, but quite another to be needed. Fred had given her both compliments in the last ten seconds.

Fred pattered her shoulder, "Come on. Let's get inside."

Jo stripped out of her rain gear and hung it on the hook. She'd heard the engine disengage, could feel the slow rock, and knew that Keller had descended to the galley, probably to assign driving to either Fred or Graham so he could yell at her for starting the fight that ended with Pete hitting the water.

Memories of the splash, the siren, and the men screaming flickered through her mind, and sent her stomach to sloshing back and forth like the boat. She gripped the wall and swallowed hard.

There was enough near-death in her normal life. Why had she come out here to have more laid out in front of her?

After another moment passed and Keller hadn't shown his face, she decided to continue as she had learned on the boat—man up—and join the rest of the crew in the galley.

In the corner of the booth, she found Pete wrapped in two wool blankets. Dry thermal underwear was visible where the blanket barely came together and one hand cradled a steaming mug just below his chin.

Keller sat next to him, taking Pete's blood pressure on his free arm.

Any inquiry about Pete's condition might seem insincere. It wasn't a huge secret how they felt about each other but it was the human thing to do. "How are you feeling?"

"Like I cheated death."

"Well, you haven't yet," Keller interrupted. "I don't like how low your pressure still is. Finish that coffee and someone make him a bowl of soup. After you eat that, I want you to get in your bunk with as many extra blankets as we have on board." Keller slid to the edge of the seat and pushed himself to his feet. "I'm going to turn us toward town. You need to get into the clinic."

"I don't need a doctor," Pete said. "We all need you to drop the bad omen on the dock though, before one of us comes up dead."

Keller twisted back. "She saved your life! Jo's the one who spotted you."

"I wouldn't have gone overboard in the first place if she hadn't started her shit out there."

"Cut the crap."

"Come on, Kell! It's time to lose the chick, so us men can get back to real fishing."

Keller leaned across the table, his hands gripping the edge. The muscles in his arms rippled, and even though Jo couldn't see his face, she was sure his left eye twitched. "Jo is a member of this crew. Don't forget that. She's not getting dumped on the docks, and if you have a problem with that, maybe you should stay on shore. If anything caused you to go overboard, it was because you spend too much time thinking about stupid-shit and not enough time concentrating on your job. Drink your coffee. Eat some soup. Get your ass in bed."

Keller then pushed off the table and sidled past Fred, exiting the galley. "Somebody bring me up some coffee and somebody else start dinner."

* * * *

In the wheelhouse, he dropped into his captain's chair and picked up the stale pack of cigarettes he hadn't had the strength to throw out. He'd pushed one out of the paper and cellophane and transferred it between his lips before he'd realized stress had backed him into the old habit.

As he reached for a lighter, the confirmation that he didn't want to end up like his father cut through his tense muscles. He pulled the smoke from his mouth and crumbled it in his hand. Unclenching his fist, he watched the paper and tobacco flutter down to the trash can, then cursed aloud.

The memory of Pete's body tumbling overboard replayed in his head. Then again, except this time it was Jo's body flipping over the rail. He clenched his fist and squeezed his eyes tight, forcing the image from his mind. "Get your fucking head back in the game."

A soft touch to his shoulder turned him around. He gazed into Jo's eyes for a moment, digging deep for the words to say, but fear balled up in his throat, making it hard to breathe, let alone talk.

She set his coffee cup on the ledge by his chair, and then said, "Everything's okay."

At her words, he stood and pulled her into his embrace, squeezing her as tight as possible, and burying his head in her hair.

She returned his affection, tightening her arms around his waist and kissing his neck.

"You're trembling," he whispered, then gently kissed her temple.

"Everyone told me, over and over, but it...it didn't seem real."

He lifted her chin so he could kiss her mouth. "You were remarkable. You stayed calm and did what needed to be done."

Her cheeks reddened and he couldn't help smile. Jo had dropped the walls she hid her vulnerability behind. She trusted him. "I'm just glad you were able to get to him, and that Graham and Fred were able to get him out of the water."

He kissed her forehead again and then pulled her tight once more.

"Another early trip to town is really going to hurt your bottom line."

"Yes, but that's not more important than Pete's life. Or yours."

"I'm fine. So is Pete."

"His blood pressure's still low."

Footfalls sounded on the steps, and both Keller and Jo turned toward the door as Pete appeared at the top of the steps. "I don't want you to head in. I want to fill the tanks first. I'm going to be fine."

Keller rubbed his temples and held his tongue, giving the emotional storm swirling in his gut a chance to settle. Pete was standing in front of them, looking mostly like himself, but that didn't mean he was out of the woods. His health could go south quickly.

Keller flipped his attention from Pete to Jo, and then back again. "Are you sure?"

"I'm positive. I still feel like a damn popsicle, but I'm okay."

He pushed his hands to his temples and tried to tune out all the voices rattling in his head. The voices of his father telling him nothing mattered more than properly running the boat. The screams of his crew searching for Pete in the water and the voice of his own conscience that said he'd never be good enough to manage the company or good enough for Jo.

"Okay...okay." He stood and stepped aside. "But, you can't go back on deck till you warm up. Go put some layers on. You're driving. I'll take your place on deck."

Pete stepped back as if Keller's words had been a shove. "What do you mean?"

Keller reached out and grabbed Pete's forearm. "We have five more pots on this string and one final string to pull today. I can certainly work on deck for that long.

"I'm not a captain."

It was probably the most humble thing Pete had ever said in Keller's presence. "I didn't say you were. I said you were driving the boat. I'll be in charge from the rail."

He started for the steps, but Jo grabbed his arm. "What are you doing?"

"Filling the boat. Let's go."

Jo started to follow Keller down the steps when Pete called her name. She turned her back.

"Thank you."

Knowing what it had taken for Pete to even mutter those words, Jo just nodded to him. There was no reason to focus on her part in his rescue. What she'd done, she'd do for anyone.

Outside the deck door, Keller and Jo caught up with the rest of the crew getting back into their gear.

"Are you sure you want to do this?" Graham asked.

"Yes! I'm sure." Keller snapped as he pulled on boots and then grabbed a bright yellow jacket from a hook on the wall. "I'm going to be on hydros. I can direct everything from there. Norm, you step over into Pete's position, and we'll be all-good." Once geared up, Keller leaned against the wall, and pressed the intercom button. "You've got the best view point, Pete. Keep the boat pointed toward the buoys and let Fred and I know what we need to know but can't see from this view point. Slow and steady, we'll get these last thirty-five pots pulled."

A shaky, and nowhere-near-self-assured voice came back over the speaker saying, "okay."

* * * *

As Keller stepped into position, he had no choice but to push away the last few weeks and months, and hush the naysaying voices. If he thought leading the boat from the wheelhouse was tough, it was going to be ten times harder to do it from this position.

Yet, it was even more important that he be ever-vigilant.

Gaining that keen focus was easier than he thought it would be and within just a couple of pots, that machine-like groove he'd spent two weeks of the season searching for was there. Everyone in the exact place they were supposed to be at every moment.

Pots coming up.

Crab going in the tanks.

Pots being baited and dumped.

A beautiful, well-oiled, efficient machine.

For a while, he felt joy again. Felt like he used to about the boat and his career. Felt as though fishing was more than a job, but what he was meant to be doing. Then, he got a good look at Jo's eyes.

They were glazed over. Her shoulders drooped, and her back hunched. He remembered the setups she'd been hauling back and forth, with what seemed like such ease, weighed forty pounds each—at best.

The soft flesh of her cheeks looked chapped by the icy breeze, and her hands trembled as she helped to sort the crab. But, she continued to push on—as she'd done the whole time, without whining.

From the comfort of the captain's seat, all he'd been able to really see, was her doing the job. He hadn't seen the toll it was taking on her. He'd forgotten she was doing it with one, sole purpose in mind—to earn the money to save her house.

So, they'd fallen into this crazy little relationship. They created a connection, had bonded over their similar life paths. As wonderful as it was, it wasn't a strong foundation. A normal relationship might be able to be built on what they had, but could they make this work, when her biggest desire was to have the house, the picket fence and the man with a nine to five and his reality was the furthest thing from her dream.

When the last pot was reset. He tapped Jo on the shoulder. "Go inside. We'll finish up out here."

She shot him a dagger-bearing glance. "I'll go in when we're done."

The boat slowed way down, and Keller realized Pete needed instruction. He crossed to the intercom by the door and pressed the button. "Turn for string one."

CHAPTER TWENTY

Jo stripped out of the gear and made her way to the galley, grateful that it was Norm's turn to cook. She slid into the booth and balanced her head in her hands, her wobbly legs thankful for the rest.

As smooth as everything had gone on deck, Keller set a pace that had proved difficult to keep up with.

He'd disappeared up the steps to the wheelhouse, and when she heard footfalls coming back down, assumed he'd relieved Pete, until Keller grabbed her arm. "Come with me."

She had to dig for the strength to get her feet under her, but then followed him around the corner. When he opened the door to his cabin, she pulled back and shook her head.

Keller gently tugged on her hand. "I don't care what anyone thinks anymore."

Jo relented. He gave the door a harder than necessary push and it slammed it shut. Then, pressing Jo against the wall, he held her there with his body, deeply kissing her.

Taken by surprise, she stiffened, but then melted into him, wrapping her arms around his neck.

"What if it had been you? I haven't been able to shake that image from my mind," he mumbled against her lips.

"But it wasn't."

"I was so stupid." He gripped her hair in his hands. "You could have been hurt."

She pressed against his shoulder. "I'm not. This job has been the hardest thing I've ever had to do, but I have done it."

His fingers traced her jawline. "But you shouldn't have to."

"Don't say that. You sound like my father." She tried to push passed him, but he shifted his weight using his body to block her exit.

"I don't say that because you're a woman, I say that because I care about you. Today, for the first time, I saw how really difficult every step across the bow has been for you."

"I didn't complain!"

"Not for a second. And that's what makes you so special, but that doesn't mean I *want* you to do it."

She laid her head on his shoulder, let him pull her to him, let him support her body. Her muscles melted as the stress washed from them. "We'll be done soon. Right?"

"One more day. The tanks will be full, and you'll be done. You hit the mark."

She tried to run the numbers through her head. Yes, this second trip had run smooth as silk until Pete had tumbled overboard. Keller had put them on good fishing and they'd been hauling nothing but full pots.

Still, the idea that she'd gone from barely making a scratch to earning enough to pay off the loan in those five days seemed impossible.

Keller moved them a few steps back toward the bed. He sat on the edge and guided her to his lap. Pushing her hair off her shoulder, he kissed her neck. "I'm going to miss having you here."

She leaned her temple to his, and couldn't stop the soft laugh. "I'll miss you too, but I won't miss being on this boat."

He tipped her chin in, brushing his lips to hers. "I said that once. Thought I was walking away for good, but, you know. Being a fisherman isn't what I do. It's who I am."

His fingers traced up and down her spine, and she laid her head on his shoulder. She'd realized a week ago what Keller now knew. For a brief moment she tried to tell herself he might change for her, but when it came down to it, she knew she wanted him for who he was. Even if that was a fisherman.

So sensual. The opposite of the rock-steady guy who was in command of his boat. She leaned into him, wanted to lie down next to him.

He slid a hand down her arm and gripped her wrist. "Not like this. Not with those boneheads on the other side of the door."

She knew he was right and tried to push down her desire. "Can you stay a night with me in town?"

A slow, sumptuous kiss that made her toes curl answered the question. When the kiss broke, he nibbled at her ear before whispering, "Only if we can repeat the last time."

"You think you're up to it?"

He laughed and laid his hand against her cheek. "I don't want to go out there. I want to stay right here, like this, with you, but Pete needs to get some rest."

"And I should check in with my mom and dad and let them know when I'm coming home."

* * * *

As Jo followed Keller out of his cabin and started up the steps to the wheelhouse she heard rumblings in the galley. Though none of the words were clear, she could imagine it had to do with her and Keller.

The last thing she had wanted the guys to think was that she stayed on the boat because of her relationship with the captain, but knowing that it was all but over made it less troublesome to her.

Picking up the satellite phone, she dialed her mom without even thinking about it. When her mother answered, she got straight to the good news. "I'm almost done, one more day of fishing and then a day of travel. Will Dad be ready to come home soon?"

"Actually, yes, I should be bringing him home the day after tomorrow too."

"Bringing? That's not necessary, is it?" In recent calls to her mother, she'd felt like she was getting half-truths. Now, she was sure of it. "Why can't he travel alone?"

"He probably could, but I promised him I would make the trip with him. Once I get him to you…I'm catching up with Ben and the kids in Oregon."

Her mom paused, but Jo couldn't shake the feeling of a dark cloud. "What are you not telling me?"

"Don't get mad, Jo."

"Mom?"

"When I got here to Anchorage, I had a long talk with your father about how he's kept you chained to him."

Frustration mounted. What would she have to do to get her mom to drop this idea that she clung to. "What are you talking about?"

"We both agreed that he would go through this treatment without leaning on you."

"What the hell? What went wrong?"

Her mother exhaled loudly into the phone, and Jo could visualize the look that must be on her face, that patented mother-knows-best glare. "Take a deep breath. He's fine. He's going to be great. You both needed to do some enduring alone."

Jo pushed her fingers through her hair, gripping the locks. She started to count to ten, grab a hold of the temper that often got her in trouble with her mom, but it was no use. "Put my father on the phone!"

"Jolanda!"

"Either tell me what's going on, or put Dad on the phone," she insisted.

"I'm not at the hospital. I'm back in my hotel for the night."

There was a long pause. Jo remained silent, giving her mom room to explain. Just when she thought she couldn't wait another minute, her mom continued. "The doctor in Unalaska had warned you he might lose a couple of toes. It really isn't uncommon for someone in his condition."

Someone in his condition. "Don't do that. Don't try to put distance between me and him. He's my father. And you should have told me. You had no right to keep it from me."

"You're over reacting. It took two surgeries, but everything is healing nicely now."

"Two surgeries! He went through two surgeries without me there! As soon as my feet are on dry land, I'm going to be on a plane to Anchorage!"

"By the time you would get here, we'd be there. He's being released tomorrow, and I have a flight booked for the day after. The only reason I'm coming is because he's still a little unsteady on his feet."

"You let me know what time the plane comes in and I will meet you at the airport. That way you can get on a plane back to your *real* family as quick as possible."

Jo heard her mother calling her name again as she disconnected the phone.

"I can't believe she did that to me. She's always accusing my father of trying to control me and keeping me tied to him, but she's the manipulative one."

Keller took her hand and squeezed it. "What happened?"

"They had to take a couple of toes, I guess. She never said exactly, just that he needed two surgeries."

"But he's okay now."

"Yes, or so she said, but that's not the point. Every time I called she would tell me he was fine, and she kept him from telling me the truth. Remember, I've said he's sounded distant with me."

"But he *is* fine."

"I should have been there! My father needed me and I should have been there!"

CHAPTER TWENTY-ONE

Exhaustion had set in. Emotional. Physical. Pure exhaustion.

This sunrise had marked the eighth he'd watched with no more than the occasional cat-nap. The last time Keller had felt like this was the morning after his father's funeral.

They'd burned through the last day of fishing, and the bounty was plentiful. Jo said she welcomed the work, and he knew it was because it served as a distraction.

She'd spent most of the night keeping him company before he'd been able to convince her to get some sleep in his cabin.

He would lay money, she hadn't slept though. He knew damn well what she was feeling. The words she said and the emotion she'd said them with had replayed through his mind over and over all night long.

My father needed me, and I should have been there!

Keller shut down the engines and stood. From the window he watched his crew, that magical machine he'd hoped would come together, had finally melded to include Jo.

He didn't even notice that usual awkward tension between Pete and her.

With each step Keller took down to the galley and then out to the deck, he became more and more in awe of Jo's strength and felt more and more guilt for keeping her away from her father.

He'd known how quickly life comes and goes and how he regretted not being there when his dad had passed, yet, he'd encouraged Jo to go on the boat with him and not fly to Anchorage to be with Lark.

Pete and Norm had climbed down into the tanks to begin filling the bailers. Jo stood at the ready with the clipboard and pen to track the weights. The perfect job for her, but not one he wanted her doing right now. Keller came up behind her and took the clipboard from her hand, wrapping an arm around her waist as he did. He leaned in and whispered in her ear. "Go home."

She twisted her way out of his hold. "I'll go home when the job's done. And don't do that while I'm working."

He tugged on her shoulder, guiding her to look at him. "What are you talking about?"

"When the crew's working, I'm crew and you're my boss." She forced a smile that did nothing to hide how weary she was.

"I told you the other night that you're done. These guys can do the offload, you need to be with your father."

"His plane doesn't come in until this afternoon. That's eight hours, and I'd rather keep myself busy."

Arguing with her was an exercise in futility, he'd yet to win a disagreement. He let go of the paperwork, giving her both access to the job and his reluctant approval. He twisted his hand and looked at his watch. "I want you off this boat an hour before his plane lands so you have plenty of time to get over there and meet him."

Her eyes dropped and her shoulders folded. "Thanks, Kell."

He stepped closer, speaking low. "I'll come by your house later."

She nodded. "For dinner. For now, you were up all night. You should go sleep."

* * * *

Keller's hand touched the door, but then he pulled it back. He wiped the sleep from his eyes again, and pushed his fingers through his hair.

When Graham had knocked and announced that Jo's mom was on the boat and wanted to talk to him, a hundred scenarios ran through his mind—none of them good.

He took a deep breath and pushed himself forward, rounding the corner and entering the galley.

The woman looked very much as she had the night he'd seen her in the Elbow Room with Jo. Refined and self-assured; at ease with herself, but not at all with the surroundings.

Keller offered her his hand, "Mrs. ..."

What the hell is her married name?

Jo had never mentioned.

Instead of taking his hand, she waved hers in front of her face, and shook her head. "Elle. Elle is fine. And this isn't really a social call."

He shoved the rejected hand into his pocket and slid into the seat across from her. If it wasn't social, he'd forgo offering her coffee. Both of Jo's parents had now come to his boat on a serious note. That didn't bode well for a one-day big happy family he'd been day dreaming about lately. "What can I do for you, then?"

"You have quite the operation, don't you?"

Keller didn't like her tone, and squared his shoulders. Say all she wanted about him, but he was damn proud of the family business. "My father built it from the ground up, but I really don't think you're here to discuss that either."

"I gathered from all my phone conversations with my daughter that she's grown quite fond of you."

That brought a smile to his face, and to his amazement, he felt his cheeks warm slightly. "I think she's wonderful."

"She is. And as far as I'm concerned she's been wasting her life in this, this, this…taking care of her father. When I was down here a few weeks ago, I thought I had her convinced to move to Oregon with me and go to college. Now she's found another reason to stay tied to this town, her father, and the fisheries." She waved her hands around her head, making it abundantly clear she was not impressed by what he had to offer her daughter.

"What are you trying to say to me? That I'm not good enough for Jo?"

"No. Not at all, but I spent six years married to a fisherman. I know what it's like."

Keller could feel his hands tightening into fists under the table. Even though a piece of him believed Elle had a point, he resented her attacks. "My mother spent almost thirty years with my father before he died, and she didn't have a problem."

"Jo deserves the one thing Lark and I could never give her, a stable home in a single place. I hated her having to fly back and forth, not to just two separate homes, but to two different worlds. It affected her. She was a moody child; a sullen teen; and, at times, a bitter adult. Now she's become a caregiver to Lark, who—by the way—doesn't need someone to take care of him. He just likes keeping her away from me."

"You do know she's more than capable to make her own decisions about all of this. Don't you?"

"How is a relationship even going to work for you two? When you're not on this boat, where's home?"

"Everette, Washington."

"If I can't get her to leave Lark and come to Fairbanks or Oregon to go to school, do you think she's going to leave Unalaska for you?"

He shrugged his shoulders. "I didn't ask her to. Maybe I'll move up here." Soon as the words slipped by his lips he knew that was an idea that would never work.

She shook her head. "You forget that Lark was working for your father when I was married to him. You only run these boats out of this port about three months a year, the other nine you're down there. Hal used to try to talk Lark into coming down there to fish all the time. Talked him right into it one year, the year I took Jo and moved out."

"Jo is not you." He continued to argue even though the voice in his gut told him Elle was right. Jo had never given him an ultimatum like Brie had. But that didn't mean Jo wouldn't ask him to make a choice one day. He'd learned once that walking away from the boats was an impossibility. If he came to the same conclusion with Jo, would she leave him too?

Just like Brie had left him.

Just like Elle had left Lark.

Maybe his mother was the exception, not the rule.

"How many days a year are you on a boat, Keller?"

He pushed himself away from the table. "You know what, all of this is between Jo and me. We'll figure it out."

"And then what? My baby has already wasted too much time being stagnant; working in a cannery, caring for her father. Let's say she spends another year or two trying to make it work with a wanderer like you—"

"*Wanderer?* What the hell is that supposed to mean?"

Elle stood and grabbed her purse from the seat next to her before zipping her jacket and wrapping the delicate silk scarf around her neck. "All I'm saying is before you steal what's left of her youth, take a few minutes to think about what's best for her. Don't string her along because it's what's best for you."

* * * *

After Elle left the boat, Keller thought about going back to bed, but was too worked up to sleep.

How dare she?

Even if she thought she was protecting Jo, Elle must have a brass pair to interfere in their lives like that.

So, instead of going back to his cabin, he layered up his clothing and went out on deck to supervise what was left of the cleanup.

No matter how hard he worked, or how much he busied himself, the words *Jo deserves better than this, better than you* kept playing through his head.

As they were finishing the work, Keller thought he might be tired enough to get a little bit of sleep before heading over to Jo's. He'd just stripped off his parka and his wool sweater when he heard the chime to his phone alerting him to a text.

He pushed the buttons and clicked on the icon that displayed his brother's picture. His fears of bad news, were washed away when the image of a small baby, wrapped in a blue blanket, flashed on the screen accompanied with the words, "It's a boy."

Keller no sooner absorbed the idea that his brother's son had made it to the world—healthy and happy—despite the recent threats, when several other texts began streaming into his phone, more pictures, from every member of his family.

More reminders that a wonderful family moment had just happened, and he was far away from home, unable to participate.

CHAPTER TWENTY-TWO

After a nap, and thirty minutes in a hot shower, Jo felt almost human again. She followed the sounds of clatter to the kitchen and found her father putting a pan in the oven.

"Hey, you're supposed to be resting that foot."

He turned to her and smiled, carefully moving to the chair at the table. "I've been taking it easy. I promise. I know how tired you can be when you come off the boat. I didn't want you to have to worry about fixing dinner."

She sat down in the chair next to him and pushed her hair out of her face rubbing her temples. "I'm glad you're home. And I'm sorry I wasn't with you."

Lark reached out and took her arm. "Why?"

"Because you're my dad. If I had known you were going through surgery—"

"To what end, Jo? You're not a doctor. You would have been sitting at my bedside, worrying about something that you could do nothing about. I didn't necessarily agree with your mother about keeping the truth from you, but I did know that she was right about how you would have reacted. You would have got off the boat and on a plane."

"And that's wrong?"

He leaned into her. "Not wrong. Just unnecessary."

When she was fighting to work on the boat, she'd wanted everyone around her to see her as an adult, able to make her own decisions. Now, she was seeing glimpses of that in her father's eyes, and she felt herself growing even closer to him. "There's something I need to tell you, and I don't know if you're going to like it."

"You and Keller are more than friends."

She tipped her head.

How does he know?

"You're mother told me about her suspicions." He answered her unasked question. "Then, I called up Graham and asked him what was going on."

"And he can't keep anything from you."

Lark laughed. "Do you know why I've always talked up you and Graham being together?"

"Because you like him?"

"It's more than that, and more than the way you two have always gotten on so well."

The two reasons he said were the ones that made the most sense. "Then why?"

"I only realized this when I had to listen to your mom going on and on about how afraid she is that you won't come visit her down in the lower forty-eight. I think I thought if you and Graham got married and started a family, you'd always be close to me."

"Dad…" It was ridiculous that either parent would worry that Jo would just cut them off, but then, she'd been doing a version of that for most of her life. Always focused on pleasing the parent she was with at the moment the most.

Her father tapped on the center of his chest. "I've always known in here that I was being silly. I guess, the memory of coming off the boat to find you and your mom gone has never left me. I never wanted to experience that again, and neglected to see the woman you've grown to be. If I had, I'd have known you'd never abandon anyone."

"No matter what happens with Keller, I'm not going to leave you—or mom—behind."

"Wrong. You're an adult. It's time to go on and start your own life, your own family. I'm not going to lie. Being with anyone whose work takes them away from home for weeks and weeks isn't easy. It's damn hard. But, it's not impossible."

"Watching you and mom, I always thought it was."

"You are not your mother. Keller's not me. We failed, many other couples make it work. It's a hard road, baby, but you're strong enough to walk it."

What is it they say about not knowing what you want until it's right in front of you? If Jo had been asked just a few weeks ago if she wanted to date Keller, she would have dismissed him solely because of the job he did, but now that she'd spent the last couple of weeks getting to know him, all she wanted was more time to explore the relationship.

* * * *

Twenty minutes later, Jo was pulling the meal her father had made from the oven when a knock sounded on the door. She set the pan down just as she heard her father greeting Keller, and wiped her hands on the dishtowel.

In the living room, she eagerly crossed to Keller, opening her arms.

He accepted her hug, but his body was stiff and he seemed closed off.

"Are you tired?" she asked.

He nodded, and looked around the room. "Can we go out on the porch and talk, please?"

She took her coat from the hook and draped it over her shoulders before slipping into her deck shoes.

Keller was probably a little nervous about showing affection in front of her father. As soon as she explained the conversation they'd just had, he'd settle down. "Dad and I had a long talk this afternoon –"

He placed a hand on her shoulder. "I need to say this, and I need you to let me say it without interrupting me."

She nodded, tugging on the front of the coat, trying to close it.

"I've been thinking a lot this afternoon about where we go from here. And I keep coming back to the same conclusion. We're absolutely crazy. This isn't going to work."

"How can you say that?"

"How can you not see it? Your home is here, mine is in Washington. I spend weeks on end away from home, and you hate the boat. Didn't you say once that the last thing you ever wanted was a guy who was never there?"

"That was before I got to know you. I'm not saying it's going to be a cake walk, but don't you think it's worth a try?"

"What are we trying for? Another broken heart?"

Of course.

He'd been hurt so badly by Brie. "I didn't ask you to give up the boats."

"Not yet."

"Not ever. I get it. You're a fisherman. I don't want to change that."

"You say that now, but what will you say in six months when we've spent so few days together you can count them on your hands?"

Everything he was saying made sense on paper, but her heart was screaming at her to not let him slip away. "If it bothers you, I'll go out with you. I have no problem doing that."

"What? So you can get tossed over the side like Pete did? I'd never be able to live with myself if you got hurt or died on my boat." He slid a trembling hand against her cheek. "You're so strong. So bold. *So* smart. You deserve more than all this."

"Don't I get a say in that?"

"I'd rather end it now, on the good memories, than have my heart shredded when you end up hating me in a few months."

He unzipped his parka, reached inside, and pulled out a check from the breast pocket of his flannel shirt.

The last thing she wanted in this moment was his money. It felt too much like he was paying her off. She folded her arms across her chest and took a step back. "I won't let you do this. You can't just give me money and walk away."

He stepped closer to her, pushed the check into her front jeans pocket. His fingers tickling her hip bone. His breath hot on her cheek as he stood inches from her. "You earned this! I was going to just write it for what you owed the bank, but I couldn't dishonor you like that. You gave more than everything you had for the people you love, and I needed to respect you enough to pay you for the work you did. It's not quite enough, but close enough to get the bank to work with you, I'm sure."

She gripped his jacket, and held him close. "You're a coward!"

He locked his hands around her wrist. "Don't do this. Don't make it harder."

"If it's so hard, then why?"

"You deserve better than me!"

"That's bullshit. Did something happen to make you change your mind?"

His eyes closed and he tugged gently at her wrist. "Let me go. Please."

"I don't want to," she whispered. "I'm not sure what's been going on between us. I don't know if we can make it work, but I'm willing to try. Why aren't you?"

"Because I know how this story ends."

Jo let her hands fall away, and used the back of one to wipe a tear off her cheek.

Keller took two steps back before whispering, "I'm sorry." He then turned and nearly ran down the walk, climbed into his truck, and drove away without looking back.

CHAPTER TWENTY-THREE

Keller pulled the truck into the slot by the docks and twisted the key. He reached for the handle, but his hands were shaking so bad that he couldn't get the door to open.

"Damn it all!" he muttered and then slammed his hand against the steering wheel.

Breaking things off with Jo had hurt more than a grappling hook to the forehead, but it was best for her.

And Jo was the important one in all of this.

The conversation with Elle that afternoon had pissed him off at first, but when Reese sent the picture of his healthy, happy son by text, her point had been driven home.

He could imagine himself sitting at the docks and getting a text from Jo with the first pictures of their child, and that's when he knew the relationship was doomed.

She'd spent way too much time as a child moving between two homes, splitting her love and missing the parent who wasn't there, to have to spend the next phase of her life missing an absentee boyfriend or husband.

Still, watching her plead, seeing that she had the desire and strength to face her biggest fears and give it a chance, had reminded him how tenacious she was.

How resilient she was.

Keller had to show the same kind of character. He had to be strong enough to let her go.

He rubbed the back of his neck and gripped his hair,

pushing down the emotions, clenching composure with both hands for all it was worth.

As he made the walk from the truck to the boat, he kicked at the stones.

What a fool!

The second Jo had turned his head, he'd reminded himself it would end like this.

Why had he surrendered to the longing?

He was thankful that the boat was quiet. The men were enjoying their twenty-four hours off, probably at the Elbow Room.

Closing his eyes tight, he pushed away the images of her prodding him to let her on the boat. He laughed as he remembered her absurd bet.

Let me prove to you I'm strong enough to do the work. I bet I can beat you at any game.

She'd meant darts or the silly shuffle board game.

"How do you think any of that is going to prove you can handle yourself on my boat," he'd asked.

"You certainly seem to be good enough at drinking, how about I drink you under the table," she'd replied.

A ridiculous offer and his agreement to play had been just as ludicrous.

A crazy claim.

Almost as crazy as her pulling her weight and drawing his crew together.

He grabbed two beers out of the refrigerator and sat down at the table in the galley. Opening one, he took a long draw.

The boat had run without her, he'd find a way to run it that way again.

After drinking the two beers, Keller had decided food

was in order. It was going to be hard enough to head back to sea without Jo, he didn't need a hangover on top of it. He was almost done, when he heard footfalls on the deck.

He started for the door to see who was out there, when it opened and he heard Larks' voice calling his name.

He hurried around the corner, afraid the man would slip and fall, and was surprised to find him sure-footed and looking much better than the last time he'd visited him on the boat. At the house a few hours ago, Keller had been too focused on Jo to notice the improvement to Lark's condition. "What are you doing here?"

Keller could only imagine. Lark was probably on a mission to kick his ass for even attempting a relationship with his daughter, let's not forget he'd just broken up with her.

"Thought I'd come over here and see what's gotten in to you." He pointed to the table, "besides the alcohol."

"I called it off, okay. I won't see her anymore."

Lark chuckled. "Is that why you broke her heart? Because you thought I wouldn't approve."

"Everyone knows how you feel, but no. That's not it."

Lark made himself at home and slid into the bench behind the table. "So...you going to clue me in?"

The last thing Keller wanted to do was have this discussion. At least Jo's father—having been a fisherman most of his adult life—would understand. Keller pulled his cellphone out of his pocket and brought up one of the dozens of pictures he'd been sent today. After looking at the baby for a moment he handed the phone across the table. "Reese's wife had a boy today."

Lark's eyes lit up when he saw the baby. "That's

absolutely wonderful for them." He pushed the button turning off the lighted screen and handed the phone back to Keller. "And not being there made you think about everything you might miss?"

"What might? You know how it is. I know what Jo went through being split between you and your ex. She's told me how hard it was."

"So, you got a visit from Elle? I thought that might be behind your sudden change of heart."

"No offense, but she certainly is opinionated, huh?"

"She is that, but it comes from a place of love. Especially when Jo's concerned."

"And in this case, she's right."

"No, she's not."

"What would a relationship with me bring Jo but more loneliness?"

"My marriage to Elle didn't work, but the same thing happens to a lot of other marriages whose partners work normal everyday jobs. It comes down to commitment."

"So you're saying that fishing had nothing to do with your marriage disintegrating?"

"Yeah, it played a part. Of course, it did. But you are not me, and Jo's not Elle. After the divorce, I had opportunities to fish during the summer, more than I care to count, but Jo came first with me. I worked during the summer, but not at sea."

"But If I don't put my all into what my father built..."

"Stop thinking like that! Hal ran his company his way, and that worked for him. You and Reese have to do what's right for the two of you. Now, if you really don't want to try to work things out with my daughter, that's up to you. But, I sure hope that if you do care about her, you don't let fear and stupidity stand in your way."

"What about Graham?"

"I had my own selfish reasons for wanting that, but I was just as wrong as Elle. It's Jo's life, not mine. All I really want is for her to be happy. You do that for her."

Lark slid out of the booth and started for the door to the deck. "She's down at the Elbow Room with the rest of the crew. Just in case you were wondering."

CHAPTER TWENTY-FOUR

Keller walked into the Elbow Room and scanned for Jo. At the center table, he found her. Just like Lark had said, she was sitting with the guys, talking and laughing. She was one of the crew in every way but the most obvious.

She was all woman.

He approached the bar, and slid a fifty dollar bill toward the bartender asking for a fifth of whiskey and two shot glasses.

After slipping his change into his pocket and picking up the ordered items, he approached her.

Graham saw him first, and tapped Jo's arm, pointing in Keller's direction.

She turned just as he neared the table. Her smile melted and the light faded from her eyes.

Jo picked up her purse and started to leave.

He blocked her exit. "Please, let me explain."

"Explain what?" Her arms were crossed and her body was tipped away from him. Yet, she was just as beautiful as when she was smiling warmly at him.

"Please, give me a chance." He tilted his head toward an empty table in the corner and she followed. After he sat down, he filled each shot glass and slid one across the table toward her.

She looked down and then gave him a sly grin. "You acted like a big jerk."

How he adored her clear-cut, honest approach, and her strength to deliver the truth, even if it cut at him. "You were right back at your house, I was acting like a coward." He lifted up the glass, and tipped it to her, "Can I prove to you I'm man enough to run with you?"

She tried to contain it, but a giggle escaped. "I'll be honest, just a few weeks ago you were the last thing I ever would have picked for myself. Mostly, because I didn't think I wanted what my parents had, what they couldn't make work. But then I got to know you. Now, you're the only thing I want, and I'm willing to fight for it."

"Are you willing to come out and finish the season?"

Her face paled. "Do you need me too?"

"Only if you want to."

"I'm so grateful you gave me the chance to do the work, earn what I needed, and learn a whole lot about myself, but let's face it. It's not my cup of tea. I have enough to save the house. That's all I wanted. You were just a sweet bonus."

He reached across the table, and laid his hand on top of hers. "It took a lot out of you physically. You need time to recover."

"If I stay home, will you be able to finish out the season in the black?"

"We'll be okay. The *Melbourne*'s doing really well under the new captain's guidance, and we're on track for an excellent season, too."

"That's good."

"We'll be done by the holidays. I'd like you and your dad to come south and spend them with my family."

"I'll think about it, but it sounds like a good idea." She expressed caution even though she liked the idea.

She could also give some time to her mother, step father, and siblings that way.

"What's better is that if you'll agree to give me a second chance—even if I act like a bonehead from time to time—then, it doesn't matter how many crab end up in the pots, I know that this season I've already found the ultimate catch."

EPILOGUE

Eleven months later...

Jo pushed the hood back and unzipped her blue parka before making the jump from the deck to the dock. It was unseasonably warm for late October and the harbor looked like a piece of glass. A beautiful day to set out fishing, but there was work to be done first.

With clipboard in hand, she counted the boxes of bait that had been stacked and then called out for Pete to begin loading them.

"Are you going to sign the delivery slip for me, Jo?" Mr. Crandell asked.

"Certainly," she answered, completing the task and returning the canneries copy to her former boss. As she handed it back, she noticed a softness about the man she'd once thought hadn't had a heart at all.

"You look good. We miss having you at work."

"Part of me misses it too." An honest answer. For all the good changes that happened in her life in the last year, there were still regrets and memories that pricked at her near-perfect condition.

"I heard you sold the house. Didn't think I'd ever see that day."

She chuckled. "Me either. This place is still home in a lot of ways, and I'm not disappearing. When I'm here, though, we have the boat to stay on. Now that Dad has found his own apartment near us in Washington, we just didn't need the house up here anymore."

"So, the rumors are true. He's going out as engineer on the *Melbourne* this year."

"Yes. Hopefully, if all goes well, he'll have his captain's license in the next six months."

Mr. Crandell nodded, looked as though he was searching for the words to keep the conversation moving. "When are you guys shipping out?"

"The *Melbourne* left an hour ago. The *Sydney*'s headed out later tonight. I have a flight back to Everette late this afternoon."

"Oh. You're not going out?"

Keller's voice called out from the deck of the boat. "Not this trip!"

Jo turned and smiled as he stepped up to the dock and moved in behind her, wrapping his arms around her waist. "Someone has to stay home and run the company."

Keller nuzzled her cheek. "It couldn't be in better hands."

After saying their goodbyes to Mr. Crandell, Jo turned in Keller's arms and pulled him close. "I'm going to miss you."

"I know. I'm going to miss you too, but we'll get the crab as fast as we can and then I'll be home."

"Promise?"

"You know I do."

"I could always come with you." She surprised herself with the offer. As much as the conditions weren't her ideal, the draw to stay by her husband's side pulled at her stronger.

He shook his head slowly, and let his hand slide down her arm and come to rest on her stomach. "The best place for my wife and child right now is home."

She laughed. "Well you keep that image of me padding around the apartment barefoot if that makes you happy, but I'm going to be busy keeping your books in line and looking for a house. So unless you're opposed to a little Colonial with a fenced in yard right around the corner from your mother, you better fill your quota and high tail it home."

He shook his head and tightened his embrace. "I suppose I should be scared."

"But you're not."

"Nah, I can handle whatever I have to face out there, because I have you waiting for me at home."

The End

ABOUT THE AUTHOR

Constance Phillips lives in Ohio with her husband, daughter, and four canine kids where she writes contemporary romance novels and paranormal romance novels.

When not writing stories of finding and rediscovering love, Constance and her husband spend the hours planning a cross-country motorcycle trip for the not-so-distant future...if they can find a sidecar big enough for the pups.

MORE BOOKS BY CONSTANCE PHILLIPS

FAIRYPROOF SERIES
FAIRYPROOF
COUNCIL COURTSHIP (NOVELLA)
CHASING POWER (COMING IN 2015)

RESURRECTING HARRY SERIES
RESURRECTING HARRY
LIZ'S LEGACY (COMING IN 2016)

SUNNYDALE DAYS SERIES
ALL THAT'S UNSPOKEN
ALL THAT'S UNCLAIMED
ALL THAT'S UNREALIZED
ALL THAT'S UNFORGIVEN (COMING DEC. 2015)
ALL THAT'S UNFORESEEN (COMING JAN. 2016)

ANTHOLOGY
ONE LUCKY NIGHT (LEXI'S CHANCE)

BOXED SET
SWEET BUT SEXY BOXED SET (INC. ALL THAT'S UNSPOKEN)

.

www.ingramcontent.com/pod-product-compliance
Lightning Source LLC
Chambersburg PA
CBHW031333170626
46807CB00002B/683